DOCTOR WHO

WILD BLUE YONDER

THE CHANGING FACE OF DOCTOR WHO
The cover illustration of this book portrays the Fourteenth DOCTOR WHO,
whose physical appearance mysteriously resembled that of his tenth
incarnation

WILD BLUE YONDER

Based on the BBC television adventure
Wild Blue Yonder by Russell T Davies

MARK MORRIS

BOOKS

BBC Books, an imprint of Ebury Publishing
20 Vauxhall Bridge Road
London SW1V 2SA

BBC Books is part of the Penguin Random House group of companies whose
addresses can be found at global.penguinrandomhouse.com

Doctor Who is produced in Wales by Bad Wolf
with BBC Studios Productions.

Executive Producers: Russell T Davies, Julie Gardner,
Jane Tranter, Phil Collinson & Joel Collins

First published by BBC Books in 2023

www.penguin.co.uk

A CIP catalogue record for this book is available from the British Library

ISBN 9781785948466

Editorial Director: Albert DePetrillo
Project Editor: Steve Cole
Cover Design: Two Associates
Cover illustration: Anthony Dry

Typeset by Rocket Editorial Ltd

Printed and bound in Great Britain by Clays Ltd, Elcograf S.p.A.

The authorised representative in the EEA is Penguin Random House Ireland,
Morrison Chambers, 32 Nassau Street, Dublin D02 YH68

Contents

This book is dedicated to Paul Simpson
for his friendship and support.

And to the memory of the guvnor, Terrance Dicks.

Prologue:
Apple

Isaac's head was buzzing with ideas. In fact, *so many* ideas were swirling around in there that his skull felt like a wasps' nest.

He had sat at his desk long into the night, the manuscript on which he was feverishly working lit only by the flame of a dwindling candle. By the time he laid his quill aside, wax was pooling on the desk's wooden surface. But Isaac knew that if he had stopped to stem the flow, the delay might well have stemmed his flow of ideas too, and that would never have done.

In the event, he had completed his paper – *De analysi per aequationes numero terminorum infinitas*, a snappy title if ever there was one – at a little after 3a.m., whereupon he had collapsed into bed, exhausted but content. Now the summer's day was rewarding him with bright sunshine, piercingly blue skies and clouds that were dabs of the purest white.

Exiting the main door of Woolsthorpe Manor, his family home in the Lincolnshire hamlet of Woolsthorpe-by-Colsterworth, Isaac almost collided with the housekeeper, Mrs Merridew, who was sweeping the front step.

Plump and red-cheeked, Mrs Merridew stepped back, beaming at Isaac. ''Tis a glorious day, sir!' she declared.

Isaac beamed back at her. 'England at its finest! I think, perhaps, I shall hie me to yonder apple tree, there to contemplate the mysteries of God's universe.'

Mrs Merridew wagged a finger at him. 'Well, don't come back till you've had a very good idea, sir!'

'I shan't,' Isaac said, laughing. 'Good day, Mrs Merridew.'

The apple tree was a huge and ancient thing. Its branches erupted from the thick, gnarled trunk and twined every which way like a thousand petrified tentacles. It was, without doubt, the matriarch of the orchard, and Isaac had felt secure beneath its branches ever since he was a boy. He sat now on the warm ground, his back against the rough bark, dappled sunlight playing across his face and shoulders. The air was full of birdsong, and a pair of

Red Admirals skittered erratically by. It really was the most glorious day.

Any other young man in such bucolic surroundings, particularly one who had been up half the night working, might have allowed himself the luxury of a summer doze, but not Isaac. Even now, he could feel new ideas clamouring in his skull, eager for release. He withdrew his quill, a small pot of ink and a roll of parchment from his jacket pocket. And then...

'Ow!'

An apple bounced off his head.

Ruefully Isaac rubbed the sore spot on his skull. But as he looked at the offending piece of fruit on the ground beside him, he felt a rising sense of epiphany. He reached out and picked up the apple.

'Of course,' Isaac breathed.

New and ever more exciting ideas forming in his mind, he gripped the apple harder and stared at the branches above him. But before he could transfer his thoughts from brain to parchment, the peace of the day was shattered by a monstrous cacophony of noise, like the bellowing screech of a thousand crazed harpies.

An instant later, a hellish wind sprang up out of nowhere, and Isaac looked wildly around, certain that the world was about to split in two. With horror, he saw that away to his left a large, dark shape – a crate or a box of some sort – was spinning wildly through the air towards him. The box swooped and dipped as it hurtled in his direction. And then – *WHUMPH!* – it crashed into the apple tree.

Shaken loose by the impact, dozens of apples rained down from the tree around Isaac. Some bounced off his head and shoulders as he leaped to his feet and spun round to fully take in the astonishing spectacle before him.

The box, tall and blue and seemingly made of wood, was nestled in the branches of the tree some ten feet above his head, tilted over at an obtuse angle. Alarmingly, it was straining and groaning and shuddering, like some injured bird.

'Odd's bodkins,' Isaac muttered. 'What the devil…?'

And then the lid of the box, clearly a door of some sort, flew open. Black smoke boiled out in a cloud, and then not one but two people popped up from the box and looked down at Isaac. One was a skinny man in an oddly patterned, tight-fitting suit, whose hair stuck up at odd angles. The other was a woman with long, coppery hair and a peculiarly gleeful expression. Both had soot-blackened faces.

Ever alert to new ideas, Isaac's attention turned quickly from the two strangers to the extraordinary device that the man was holding. It was the shape of a stone tablet, but made of some sleek and unidentifiable material, its surface inset with an array of square buttons. A multitude of strange strings trailed from the 'tablet' into the depths of the smoking box.

Before Isaac could organise his thoughts, the man said, 'Sorry. We're just slightly out of control. My friend, Donna – this is Donna, Donna Noble…'

The woman, Donna, gave a cheery wave. 'Hi!'

'… she dropped some coffee into the console…'

'But don't worry,' Donna interrupted. 'He's got a time machine, which means he can blame me for all eternity.'

The skinny man rolled his eyes. But despite the smoke, he didn't really look angry, or even exasperated. He actually looked as if he was *enjoying* himself.

'I just need to triangulate,' he said to Isaac, stabbing at the square buttons on his 'tablet'. 'Could you tell me what year this is?'

'It's 1666,' Isaac murmured, bemused.

The man looked momentarily alarmed. 'Oh. Stay away from London.' Then his eyes narrowed and he stared harder at Isaac, as if fully registering his presence for the first time.

'Wait a minute. Apple tree, apple, man holding apple in 1666. Are you ... Sir Isaac Newton?'

Isaac blinked. '*Sir* Isaac?'

The man's eyes widened. 'Oh. Not yet. Spoilers.'

Donna, looking delighted, turned to her companion. 'Have you got the controls set to famous or what?'

He flashed her a look. 'If I *had* controls, thank you.'

Donna turned back to Isaac with a widening grin. 'It's got to be said, *Mr* Isaac Newton, that you – above all others – can appreciate—'

The skinny man raised a finger. 'No, don't.'

Stubbornly she continued: 'You can appreciate—'

'Really, don't.'

She elbowed her companion playfully. 'Oh, come on. That you can appreciate ...'

Then suddenly the two people from the box were *both* grinning at him. Together, jubilantly, they cried out, ' ... the *gravity* of the situation!'

The explosive bang that rose from the box sounded to Isaac almost like a roar of disapproval. More black smoke billowed out – and was that a lick of flame?

Perhaps so, for the man looked suddenly alarmed.

'Oh-sorry-gotta-go-bye!' he yelled, and ducked back into the box.

Before Isaac could react, the shuddering, groaning crate tore free from its cradle of branches and spun up and off to the west, trailing shreds and splinters of wood. Above the trumpeting bellow that accompanied its departure, he heard – thought he heard – a long, drawn-out wail of distress, or perhaps excitement, from the box's two extraordinary inhabitants. Then the lid of the box slammed shut with a bang, and the next second the apparition vanished, as though it had never been there at all. Isaac was left alone on the grass, surrounded by apples, in the shade of the now somewhat battered but still redoubtable old tree.

What had just happened? Had he experienced some form of vision, or visitation? He might have thought it a dream if not for the debris the impossible box had left in its wake.

Somewhat dazed, he held up the apple still clutched tightly in his hand and stared at it.

'What was that delightful word?' he murmured, trying to recall the phrase that the two visitors had shouted in unison. 'Shavity? Havity?'

Then it came to him and he grinned in triumph.

'Mavity!'

Fenslaw

The TARDIS was on fire.

It careered through the time vortex like a cat with a burning tail, flames spiralling around its outer shell, its roof light a fierce white torch, trailing energy. The sound of its ancient engines was like the screaming of a soul in unbelievable pain.

It flickered in and out of existence, seeking egress from the vortex.

Seeking somewhere to settle, to recover…

Or perhaps to die.

It was the plainest, most undistinguished room imaginable. Small, square, empty, its grey metal walls and floor the colour of gloomy forgetfulness.

It was quiet too. The sort of quiet that was *embedded*. The room gave the impression that nothing had happened in it for years, centuries, perhaps even aeons.

The arrival of the TARDIS changed all that in an instant. It materialised neither gradually nor gracefully, but with a screaming roar, tearing a box-shaped chunk out of the metal wall behind it. Flames lapped in rippling circles around its roof as it shuddered into solid view and then almost immediately faded, as though struggling for a foothold. Finally it became dark and solid once more, yet still fire rippled around it, its roof light gouting flame like a Roman candle. The instant it was fully solid, the door flew open, and the Doctor and Donna staggered out, choking and gasping, black smoke billowing after them.

After a few steps, Donna stopped and turned back to face the stricken time machine.

'I am never. *Ever*—'

'Out of the way!' yelled the Doctor.

Throwing himself forward, he wrapped his arms around her and rugby-tackled her to the floor. A split second later, both TARDIS doors blasted outwards, and the space where Donna had been standing was occupied by a blazing inferno, which erupted from the ship as if propelled by a giant flamethrower.

Pressed to the floor, shielded by the Doctor's body, Donna was astonished not so much by the flames, which were now boiling across the opposite wall, turning it black, but by the soaring, rousing song that accompanied it. It was a song she recognised, and the way it came bellowing out of the TARDIS made her think of boy racers back home in Chiswick, blasting the eardrums of passers-by with hip hop from their car speakers.

She had barely registered the sheer, ludicrous incongruity of the situation when – *Schwup!* – the gushing wall of flame was suddenly sucked back into the TARDIS, as if time had gone into reverse. As the fire disappeared, so the music stopped too, abruptly cut off. Then the TARDIS doors slammed shut, leaving nothing behind but their dissipating echoes.

After a moment, the Doctor and Donna rose unsteadily to their feet. Stunned, blinking, brushing smuts from her clothes, Donna looked at the scorched metal wall opposite the TARDIS doors and then at the TARDIS itself. The familiar police box shell was badly singed, its windows cracked by the heat, its roof lamp blackened and smoking.

Hesitantly she asked, 'Is it … is it all right? Is it broken? Is it knackered?'

'Um …' said the Doctor and gave her a long look.

Donna suppressed a shudder. She knew exactly what that look meant. If the TARDIS *was* knackered …

As the Doctor tentatively opened the door of his ship and poked his head inside, she thought of her family waiting at home: Shaun her husband, and Rose her daughter. Mum and Gramps…

Earlier today she had been with them, blissfully unaware, and – it had to be said – pretty damn happy, going about her normal life, when… *wham!* Everything had been turned upside down by the sudden reappearance of her old friend, the Doctor – who just happened to be a Time Lord from a distant planet, and who trailed trouble in his wake as a wedding car trails old tin cans on bits of string.

Thinking about it now, she couldn't believe she could've forgotten both him and all the amazing adventures they had shared. But then, during an encounter with his old enemies the Daleks, she had absorbed all of his Time Lord knowledge, had become the DoctorDonna, and in the end he'd had to make her forget to prevent her brain from exploding with the sheer pressure of all the stuff that was packed into it.

But even so… how *could* you forget something like that? Something so momentous? So *incredible*?

The Doctor reappeared. The expression on his face was not reassuring. Even less reassuring was the way he buried his head in his hands.

'Is it bad?' asked Donna softly, not sure she really wanted the answer.

The Doctor raised his head and groaned. His voice was bleak. 'It was brand new.'

'I'm sorry.'

'Not your fault.'

'Yes, it was.' Donna took a deep breath. 'But can we fly? Can you fix it? Can we get back home?' She looked at him hopefully. If there was one thing she could rely on, it was that the Doctor always had a plan. He slipped his hands into his jacket pockets, and after a moment a slow smile crept across his face, which made Donna think of a small boy finding exactly what he'd hoped for in a lucky dip.

'We can do … anything!' he said, and held up what he'd found in his right-hand pocket. 'Sonic screwdriver.' Then he withdrew what he'd found in his left-hand pocket. 'And a non-sonic screwdriver.'

'I think a non-sonic screwdriver is called a screwdriver,' Donna pointed out.

The Doctor nodded. 'Thank you. But if I can …'

His voice trailed off as he turned back to the TARDIS, working at the lock with the ordinary screwdriver.

If you can what? Donna was about to ask, but as if he had read her mind, he suddenly began speaking again, picking up where he had left off.

' … just reconfigure. Cos this old box can

regenerate. So if I can just click it into gear…'

He frowned, listening to the internal workings of the lock with all the concentration of a safecracker trying to break into a bank vault.

'Funny thing is,' he said suddenly, 'if you drop a cup of tea into the controls, it's completely fine.'

Donna was about to ask him how often he'd done *that*, but then a more pressing question popped into her mind. 'Am I going mad, or did the TARDIS play "Wide Blue Yonder"?'

The Doctor nodded. 'It did, didn't it?'

'What for?'

'I wonder,' he mused, gently stroking the scorched outer shell of his ship, as if he might glean its secrets through touch alone.

'We sang that in the choir, in primary school,' Donna continued. 'We'd have a little concert every Christmas. But Gramps complained. He said you shouldn't be teaching children that. It sounds all jaunty and fun, but it's not. It's the military, going to war.'

'It's the air force,' said the Doctor. 'The words are *Wild* Blue Yonder. Which means the TARDIS played us a war song. Aha!'

He grinned as the lock clicked, then opened in a spiral, the metal rippling back. Pocketing the ordinary screwdriver, he produced his sonic once again and inserted it into the newly created hole, where it stuck out at a right angle. As if part of the machine itself, it began to whirr and glow gently.

'There,' said the Doctor with satisfaction. 'It can rebuild.'

But no sooner were the words out of his mouth than there was a loud clank from inside the ship, which sounded to Donna like someone dropping a tin bucket on the other side of the door. Then the TARDIS began to jolt and grind alarmingly. The Doctor stepped back, bemused.

'Oops. Okay. Yes?'

As if in answer, the TARDIS began to make what Donna could only think of as a shuddering moan – perhaps the mechanical equivalent of someone sobbing with pain. Or … no it was more than that. It had a ghostly quality to it. As if there was a restless spirit somewhere deep within the machine, wailing out its desolation and sorrow from beyond the grave. Suppressing a shiver, she glanced at the Doctor, who was staring at his old ship in fascination.

'Is it working?' she asked.

'I think so,' he said, but then rather spoiled it by murmuring, 'Strange …'

He reached out and touched the TARDIS

again. As if responding to him, the lamp on its roof suddenly blinked on and began to shine. The Doctor gave a little skip of happiness.

'There you go! Mending, mending, mending. Give it a bit of time.' He spun round, clapped his hands, eyes darting everywhere. 'So! Now! I wonder where we are? Cos that was quite a journey. We were flung across time and space. This feels like… a spaceship?'

He bent his knees, gave a little bounce, testing the conditions. Donna copied him.

'Yeah,' he said.

'Yeah,' she agreed.

'Flight,' said the Doctor.

She nodded. 'Yeah. Spaceship.'

'Let's just see.'

He turned and strode towards the only door in the room, which was as featureless as the walls around it. The door slid smoothly, noiselessly open at his approach, and the two of them stepped through it.

Oooh!

Donna thought it, but was too gobsmacked to say it. The corridor they'd stepped into was *vast*. Wide enough for at least four lanes of traffic. Tall enough to accommodate St Paul's Cathedral, and still have room to hang glide above its famous dome.

Unlike the small, square, grey room they had vacated, the corridor was a gleaming, eye-piercing white. It was cylindrical in shape, its walls lined with curved reinforcement struts that were attached at their apex to a thick support beam, which ran along the centre of the ceiling high above their heads. To Donna, the design seemed disconcertingly organic, the struts and beam like the ribs and spine of some vast creature. She couldn't help feeling she was standing in the belly of a whale – albeit a mechanical one a thousand times bigger than those they had on Earth.

Even the Doctor seemed impressed by their surroundings. 'Wow,' he breathed, spinning slowly on his heels as he looked around. 'Nice.'

'Big,' said Donna, going for understatement in the hope it would make him laugh, but the Doctor merely nodded.

'Very big.'

She tried again. 'I'd hate to be the cleaner.'

But this time he gave no indication he'd even heard her. He was peering into the distance, leaning forward as if those extra few inches would make a difference to what he could see. Donna followed his gaze, but as far as she could tell, there was no discernible end to the corridor – not in either direction, in fact. It could be a hundred miles long.

Words finally slipped from his lips: 'Is that…?'

And suddenly Donna could see it too. About… half a mile away? Standing motionless at the edge of the corridor, right where the floor met the huge, curved wall. Something taller than it was wide.

A figure?

'Hello?' the Doctor yelled, raising a hand. 'We just landed. By accident. Hope that's okay?'

Donna expected his voice to echo, to boom, but the corridor was so colossal that his words were simply swallowed by the silence.

Certainly, the 'figure', if that was what it was, hadn't heard him. Or at least gave no indication it had done so. It remained where it was. Motionless.

Donna felt a wriggle of unease. 'Is it a person or a thing?' she asked, instinctively lowering her voice.

'We could take a look?' suggested the Doctor.

'Or… we could stay here and wait for the TARDIS to mend itself, so I can get back home. My family is waiting for me.'

The look he gave her was one of both disappointment and appeal.

Donna sighed. 'Oh, all right.'

The Doctor punched the air. 'Yes!'

They started walking, and had gone no more than a dozen steps when Donna suddenly felt a prickling on the back of her neck. She glanced over her shoulder, half-expecting to see a figure darting behind a buttress, or a security camera pointing in their direction, but there was nothing.

Paranoia, she thought. *Perfectly understandable. I've just got out of the habit of doing stuff like this.*

'Still,' she said, feeling a sudden need to fill the silence, 'wherever we are, it could be worse. We've got air. We've got light. We've got mavity.'

The Doctor flashed her a curious look. Mavity? That was something to be filed away for later. 'Yeah,' he said slowly.

'Was it me,' she continued, 'or was Isaac Newton hot?'

The Doctor's reply was spontaneous and enthusiastic. 'He *was*, wasn't he! He was *so* hot!' Then he came to an abrupt halt in the middle of the corridor, a look of surprise on his face. 'Oh! Is that who I am now?'

Donna laughed. 'It was never that far from the surface, mate. I always thought—'

Before she could elaborate, they heard a sound behind them. A sound that, though familiar, rooted them to the spot.

The trumpeting grind of the TARDIS engines.

They looked at one another with horrified realisation.

'What?' Donna yelled. 'But ... no. *No!*'

Then they were running. Back along the corridor. Back towards the door to the room where they'd left the TARDIS.

It slid open accommodatingly, and they rushed inside – only to see the faintest outline of the TARDIS as it faded away.

Coliss

The Doctor leaped forward, reaching out, scrabbling at the air, as if in an attempt to haul the time machine out of the vortex and back into the here and now.

But it was too late. The TARDIS was gone, the sound of its engines dwindling to silence. All that was left to show it had been there was the police box-shaped dent it had left in the wall.

'No,' the Doctor moaned, 'no, no, no, no.'

Donna's gaze flickered between the space where the TARDIS had stood and the stricken Doctor, panic in her eyes.

'But ...' she said. 'What?'

The Doctor's shoulders slumped. He looked at her, his expression bleak. 'No,' he said again, and there was a horrible finality to the word.

Even now, Donna refused to believe the worst. Hopefully she said, 'You can get it back, though?'

And when he failed to reply: 'Doctor? You *can* get it back?'

Still he remained silent. Her voice rose, fear

making her angry. 'Doctor, you *can* get the TARDIS back, can't you? Use the sonic.'

He let out a long sigh. 'It was in the keyhole.'

Donna's mind whirled. For years her memories of travelling with the Doctor had been denied her. But now she had them back, and suddenly she recalled an adventure they had shared a long, long time ago, in a vast library on a distant planet.

'But you can whistle!' she exclaimed. 'You can snap your fingers! You can summon it! Just use that stupid head of yours and get it back!'

The look he gave her, of infinite weariness and defeat, terrified and enraged her.

'Don't look at me like that!' said Donna. 'It's your fault! I said let's stay here, but you had to wander off!'

'You wandered with me,' protested the Doctor.

'Oh, like I could stop you!'

'*You* spilled the coffee—' But then the Doctor's expression changed. The anger went out of his face. He stepped back. 'No,' he said.

And just like that, Donna's anger evaporated too. She understood the Doctor's sudden change of mood instantly and completely. They had known each other too long to be petty and vindictive, to apportion blame. Sometimes stuff happened, and they just had to deal with it.

She reached out, touched his arm. 'No,' she agreed.

'Sorry,' he said.

'No. Okay. But…' She looked around, at the grim metal room with its scorched wall, and she felt a sudden wave of dizziness, of cosmic panic. 'Oh my god. Where are we?'

She was breathing hard, almost panting. She fought hard against it, trying to calm herself.

The Doctor took her hand, gripped it tight. He raised her fist to his lips and kissed the back of it. Like a promise. A solemn vow.

Calmer now, she said, 'Rose is waiting.'

'I'll get you home,' he told her.

'How?'

'There's one hope. A mechanism, aboard the TARDIS. It's called the HADS. Hostile Action Displacement System. So if the TARDIS is in danger, it goes away.'

'Goes where?'

'Anywhere. And it only comes back when the danger is gone. I turned it off, years ago. I mean, I'd never land anywhere otherwise. I once spent three years in orbit. Then I thought, oh, turn off the HADS. But if the TARDIS is rebuilding itself, maybe it clicked back on.'

For a moment, Donna felt reassured. But then she remembered the war song the TARDIS had played. Had that been a warning? Alarmed, she said, 'But that means we've landed in the middle of Hostile Action?'

He looked rueful. 'Yeah.'

Donna looked around them, unnerved. 'There's something on this ship that's so bad the TARDIS ran away?'

This time his reply was more equivocal. 'Yes.'

She took a deep breath. 'Then –' with each word her voice rose in fury and defiance – 'we go and *kick its arse!*'

She wrenched her hand free of his and strode from the room.

Back out in the seemingly endless corridor, marching towards the 'thing', Donna yelled, 'Oi, you! Whatever you are. I want a word!'

The Doctor trailed in her wake, looking around, seemingly content to let her take the lead for now. They had been striding along at a fair old lick for five minutes, and seemed no closer to their destination, when Donna broke the silence between them.

'She was very put out. Mrs Bean.'

The Doctor looked at her, blinked. 'Mrs Bean?'

'Head of the choir. She said, it's not a war song, it's jolly. That's what she said. It's *jolly*.'

'Mrs *Bean*,' the Doctor repeated gleefully.

She glanced at him. He had a big grin on his face. And suddenly she laughed. They both laughed.

'*Fenslaw.*'

The word shocked them both. It boomed from hidden speakers overhead, echoing and robotic. Donna jerked, stopped walking, shocked into immobility. Before she could ask the Doctor where the word had come from, what it meant, the walls were moving.

It was happening all around them. Sliding, clicking movement. Like clockwork. Smooth and orchestrated. Somehow beautiful.

Donna watched with a mixture of fear and fascination, wondering if they were about to be pulled into the workings of some vast machine, their bodies mangled, pulverised.

But no. The floor they were standing on remained solid, untouched. The transformation was confined only to the curving, rib-like walls – panels sliding left and right, some falling like dominoes; buttresses and struts rotating, some disappearing into slots in the walls, while new ones, differently angled, emerged in their stead.

And then, all at once, it stopped. Leaving the walls of the corridor looking different now, but also the same. Still structurally sound, but as though they had had a redesign, a makeover.

'What was that?' asked Donna quietly.

The Doctor rubbed the side of his neck.

'Like… circuits moving? Or reconfiguring, to become …?' He grimaced, his voice trailing off.

'And what was that word?' said Donna. '*Fenslaw*? What does that mean?'

The Doctor shrugged. 'I don't know. The TARDIS translates, but now it's gone.'

She shook her head. 'No, the TARDIS translates for *me*. I thought you knew, like, twenty-seven million languages.'

'I know fifty-seven billion, two hundred and five. But not this one. Unless that was Mr Fenslaw saying his name.'

'It wasn't that,' she said with certainty.

'It wasn't that,' he confirmed.

Donna nodded towards the still-distant 'thing'. 'Jimbo didn't move. What *is* it?'

She made to move off again, but the Doctor held up a finger. 'Wait a minute. If I'm right …'

He examined the floor, a look of satisfaction crossing his face as he spotted an indented panel a couple of metres away. Marching up to it, he pressed on it with the toe of his foot, then stepped back. Next moment, two sections of floor slid silently back, exposing a gap about the size of a double bed. A platform beneath the floor rose up to fill the gap, upon which stood a chunky little vehicle – one that looked, to Donna, both futuristic and almost childishly simple.

It resembled a golf buggy for two people, but instead of wheels it hovered on a cushion of air. The controls inside it were almost toy-like, consisting of a big central steering-wheel and a gearstick.

'Your car, milady,' the Doctor said, bowing as he gestured towards it.

Instantly recognising that he was channelling the chauffeur from the old puppet show *Thunderbirds*, she grinned and replied, 'Thank you, Parker.'

They climbed in and set off, the Doctor driving, the buggy zipping along a metre or so above the surface of the floor. Donna looked around as they sped towards the 'figure', hoping to spot further clues as to where they were. The decor, though, gave nothing away, and after a minute or two she simply settled back to enjoy the ride.

It was probably three or four minutes later when they finally reached the 'thing'.

'Oh,' said the Doctor, 'it's a robot.'

He brought the buggy to a halt. They hopped out and walked over to the robot. It was about two metres tall, white, but bronzed with patches of rust. It had a round, beachball-sized head perched upon a stocky little body. Long, chimpanzee-like arms ended in big mechanical hands with chunky fingers. Stubby legs culminated in oversized, hemispherical feet.

It looked, thought Donna, both cute and sad. A row of three circular lenses inset into raised sockets on the upper part of its head resembled eyes either side of a snub nose. The outline of a flap beneath the sockets, which she guessed was there to provide access to its internal circuitry, gave the impression of a downturned mouth.

'Hello, Jimbo,' said the Doctor cheerfully. 'Can you talk? Do you have basic communications? Fenslaw? Fenslaw! Nope? *Fenslaw*. Can you hear me? Have you got controllers? Listening?' He waggled his fingers at the small, dark camera lenses that were its eyes. 'Hello? I'm the Doctor and this is Donna, and we need help. We need to – oh!'

He reared back as, without warning, the robot came to life. It took a step towards the wall it was facing, a clanking, hissing plod.

The Doctor and Donna stepped back, half-readying themselves to run, wary of what the robot might do next.

But it did nothing. After its one clanking step it came to a halt.

They waited. Five seconds. Ten.

'Is that it?' Donna said finally.

The Doctor glanced at her, raised an eyebrow. 'One step at a time.'

Donna ventured closer, looking again into the machine's sad little 'face'. 'But the robot doesn't match the ship. It's all rusty and broken. Maybe it's an invader. Maybe that's the Hostile Action.'

She looked hopeful, but the Doctor shook his head. Indicating the walls, he said, 'But it's the same metal. I think the robot's just old. It's primitive, if you don't mind me saying so, Jimbo. Someone got a very old robot out of storage, to walk very slowly down a very long corridor. Why?'

'Maybe time has slowed down,' suggested Donna.

'No. I'd feel it. In my bones.' The Doctor gave the robot a long, appraising look, then stepped back. 'Stay there, Jimbo. No sudden moves. Onwards!'

He turned back towards the buggy, but Donna hopped in front of him and slid into the driver's seat. 'I've got it.'

He shrugged and climbed into the passenger seat, beside her.

'*Allons*, as idiots say, *y*!' Donna cried.

And off they went.

The hover-buggy was ludicrously easy to drive, but Donna was still relieved when, what felt like some fifteen or so minutes later, the end of the corridor finally came into sight.

They saw it looming ahead of them a couple of minutes before they reached it – a huge, wide bulkhead wall inset with a central doorway.

She brought the buggy to a halt a few metres in front of it, and she and the Doctor hopped out and straightened up. As they did so, Donna felt that prickling sensation on the back of her neck again. She turned, certain this time there would be someone or something creeping up behind them. But all she saw was the long, white corridor stretching in their wake.

With a quick shudder, she hurried after the Doctor, who was already striding, hands in pockets, towards the door. When he was a metre away, it slid soundlessly open and he walked through. Irrationally afraid that the door might suddenly close again, trapping her outside, Donna put on a spurt of speed, and was relieved when she passed through the doorway and was standing at his side.

Looking around, she saw they were in a sort of antechamber. Dark, cylindrical corridors ran off to the right, to the left and straight ahead. Like the vast corridor they'd just vacated, the design was vaguely organic-looking, the corridors ridged in sections, like giant hollow vertebrae. The metal was grey here, though, rather than white, the lighting more subdued.

After no more than a quick glance around, the Doctor strode nonchalantly forward, hands in pockets, like a sightseer on a guided tour. Another, smaller door slid open at their approach, and stepping through it they found themselves on what Donna guessed was the flight deck – which, although small, was quietly impressive.

The first things she noticed were the glass pipes adorning the walls. Glowing with a blue, ethereal light, there were dozens of them, some arranged in intricate grids that reminded her of circuit boards, others in chunky rows that looked like avant-garde radiators. It took her another moment to realise that the faint and relaxing bubbling she could hear was water – or at least clear liquid – rushing in a constant flow through every pipe.

Turning her attention from the pipes to the

pilot's chair in the centre of the room, she saw that it was big and grey and elegantly curved, and clearly designed for a life form taller than both herself and the Doctor. Surrounding the chair was an array of hexagonal monitor screens, arranged in a honeycomb-like formation, and connected by more of the bubbling glass pipes.

In front of the pilot's chair, and accessed via a walkway on both sides, was a sweeping, oblong-shaped viewing gallery, which looked out through vast windows onto … what?

All Donna could see was blackness. A blackness that defied the eye. There was not a glint of light, not a star, not a planet. She glanced at the Doctor, who was examining the screens around the pilot's chair, gently tapping one with the tip of an index finger.

'Definitely a spaceship,' she said, then nodded at the blackness beyond the windows. 'If that's space. Or is it just night?'

The Doctor glanced at the darkness, distracted. 'Could be a cave. Or underwater.'

He turned back to the chair, seemingly more interested in the alien tech than in what was outside. Then, with a smile, he vaulted the side of the chair and flopped into it, cracking his knuckles in anticipation. 'We've got a chair,' he remarked. 'That's a good sign. It's a life form with a bum.' Entirely in his element, he began to poke and prod at the screens around him, which bleeped and burbled in response as they displayed meaningless gibberish. 'And if I can translate their basic one to ten, I can find out where we are. And when. And why.'

With seeming recklessness, he twiddled and twisted some of the bubbling pipes into new configurations before jabbing again at the screens. The gibberish began to move, alien symbols scrolling rapidly. The Doctor leaned forward, eyes flickering, his brow furrowing as he concentrated.

'One, two, three, four, five, six seven, eight, nine and ten!' he announced triumphantly less than a minute later. 'Now I can read the base codes. So …' Fingers danced, eyes flickered. Lips pursed. 'Life signs … none. Just an empty chair.'

'Where've they all gone?' Donna asked.

The Doctor now raised both hands, and began to manipulate several screens. He looked like a musician playing multiple keyboards at once. 'The ship seems to be powered down. Basic functions ticking over.' Something caught his eye on a screen to his left. 'Oh! Someone opened an airlock door. Three years ago. Then it closed.'

'Why would that happen?' asked Donna. 'Has the whole ship been empty for three years?'

'Don't know – *ooh!*' He pointed at a block of symbols. 'Those numbers are lenses. There's a camera, like a drone. We can see where we are.'

Once again, his fingers rippled across the controls.

On the outside of the ship, a circular panel slid slowly open, releasing a white metal ball with a big, staring lens at its front end. The drone hovered for a moment, like a chubby, wingless bumble bee, and then it began to whizz along the side of the ship, its lens swivelling like a cyclopean eye.

'Look,' said the Doctor, tilting a screen towards Donna, who was now leaning against the chair he was sitting in, peering over his shoulder, 'it's outside. *Whoa!* This is *definitely* a spaceship.'

The two of them stared at the screen, which gave them a drone's eye view of the ship's exterior. The vessel was huge and incredibly long, which was hardly surprising judging by the time it had taken to drive the hover-buggy all the way to the flight deck from where they'd left the TARDIS – or rather, where the TARDIS had left them.

The drone was moving considerably faster than

the buggy had, but even so it took a good while to reach the front end of the ship. From the outside, the flight deck was nothing but a black bulb, like a match-head on the tip of a particularly long match. It gave Donna a slightly vertiginous feeling to think that she and the Doctor were inside that bulb right now, watching the feed from the drone's camera.

To offset her queasiness, she asked, 'What kind of spaceship is this?'

'Don't know,' admitted the Doctor. 'But … aha!'

He tapped delicately at one of the screens, then looked up. Donna followed his gaze, and suddenly saw a dot of light appear in the blackness beyond the windows. For a split second she wondered if this was a visitor, something new, and then she realised it was simply the drone, which had circled around to the front of the ship and was now pinning them with its searchlight.

Glancing at the screen, Donna saw the Doctor sitting in the chair, and herself standing beside him with a slightly startled look on her face. Bleached by the drone's light, they looked like thieves caught in the act. The Doctor waved cheerily and shouted, 'Hello!' Instinctively Donna too raised a hand. On the screen she saw their own images waving back at them.

She felt oddly relieved when the drone zipped away, and their images disappeared from the viewing screen.

'But if we're in space,' she said, 'there's no stars. Where are the stars?'

The Doctor pushed out his lips in a facial shrug. 'We could be inside a gas cloud, or a mavity well, or... *oh!*'

Donna glanced at him. He was staring at one of the screens. Then he flopped back in the chair as if the energy had gone out of him, his expression grave.

'What?' she asked, alarmed.

He spoke quietly. 'It's fine.'

She glared at him. He caught her eye and grimaced.

'The ship,' he murmured, 'it's lost. It fell through a wormhole.'

'Ending up where?'

Still his voice was soft. As if that could cushion the blow. 'We can't see any stars because we're too far away. I'm sorry, Donna. The TARDIS was out of control, and it's taken us... to the edge of the universe.'

Wearily he stood up and stepped out of the pilot's chair. He followed the sloping walkway up and around to the centre of the viewing gallery.

Donna trailed after him. He leaned forward until his forehead was touching the glass of one of the huge, irregularly shaped windows. The drone had disappeared now, its light no longer visible, so all they could see beyond the window was an endless vista of impenetrable darkness.

'So, what's out there?' Donna asked.

The Doctor gave a huff of not-quite-laughter. 'Well. That's difficult, for you. Because if the universe is everything, then the concept of an everything having an edge is kind of impossible. But that's the language of twenty-first-century Earth. And you don't know anything yet.' When she opened her mouth to protest, he held up a hand. 'Not being rude, you just don't. When you discover Camboolian Flat Mathematics, you'll discover it's possible.'

'What's possible?'

'*That*. The nothing at the edge of creation. Absolute nothingness.'

They both looked out at the blackness. Donna thought about a saying she'd heard, something about staring into an abyss and the abyss staring back at you. She shivered and took a step back.

'We're so far out,' the Doctor said. And he sounded wistful now, full of regret. 'Past the Condensate

Reefs. Over the Realm of the Boltzmann Brains. Beyond matter. And light. And life.'

Donna hated how defeated he seemed. Yet at the same time she knew it was only his presence that was keeping her panic at bay. If she was to find herself alone here ... She pushed the thought down.

'But starlight travels,' she said. 'You can stand in my garden and look at the light from a billion miles away. So where's the light?'

The Doctor squinted, calculated. Finally, he pointed off to the right. 'Over ... there. It just hasn't reached us yet. If we flew in that direction, it would take us a hundred trillion years to reach your house.'

Donna looked in the direction he was pointing. 'That's my family,' she said in a small voice. 'Over there.'

The Doctor placed his hands on the glass and pushed, as though daring it to break. 'I've never been this far out. To stand here like this, physically unprotected, right on the edge. No one has. Not ever. Until us. And this ship.'

'And an airlock door that opened, three years ago, and closed,' Donna said.

The Doctor looked at her. 'Yeah.'

Donna sighed, and to soothe her anxiety, she tried to take solace from the calm, almost womb-like swish of water through the pipes around them. But suddenly the peace was shattered by a resounding *CLANG!* which seemed to come from the direction of the main corridor and was undoubtedly the sound of metal bashing on metal.

The Doctor and Donna looked at each other, both of their faces wearing the same expression of wide-eyed shock.

Then, without a word, they turned in unison and raced back the way they had come.

Brate

In her mind's eye, Donna was picturing a hulking, six-metre tall alien maintenance man who'd let slip a gigantic spanner from one of his many tentacled appendages. But when the automatic door slid open and they raced out into the vast, white corridor, they saw … nothing.

There was no indication anything had been disturbed. The hover-buggy remained where they'd parked it; nothing had fallen over; nothing had become detached from the walls or roof and crashed to the ground.

'Must've been just … settling,' the Doctor said unconvincingly.

'You said no life signs. Are you absolutely certain?' Donna asked.

Before the Doctor could reply, the booming, robotic voice they'd heard earlier said, '*Coliss.*'

Instantly, the walls began to reconfigure around them again. It was the same as before. Panels sliding and clicking. Buttresses and struts changing position. It lasted maybe ten seconds, and when it was over, the walls were whole once more, but had undergone another subtle alteration. Same space, slightly different decor.

Far down the corridor, unseen by the Doctor and Donna, the little robot took another slow, clanking step. Just one.

And then it stopped.

Donna let out a long breath, unaware of how tense she'd been during the 'makeover' until it was over. She looked at the Doctor, wondering if he was as unsettled by the moving walls as she was, but the only expression she saw on his face was fascinated curiosity.

'It said Fenslaw and Coliss,' the Doctor murmured. 'Like a list. Or a solicitor's. Or a countdown. Or instructions ...'

'Or a warning?' suggested Donna.

The Doctor looked at her. 'A slow warning.'

He swivelled on his heels, looking all around him. Then, coming to a decision, he headed back to the antechamber, Donna following.

Passing through the automatic door, he turned right. 'I think ... this way.'

At the end of the short corridor, they emerged into a small pod-like room, which contained more windows looking out onto blackness, and more bubbling, glowing water pipes. Instead of a pilot's chair and its attendant screens, however, this room contained what to Donna looked like rows of metal filing cabinets or specimen cases, stacked with thin vertical racks.

She watched as the Doctor pulled out one of the racks, and saw that it contained long strips of small rectangular panels divided into irregularly shaped sections, like blank frames of celluloid. The panels were coated with a sticky, golden, honey-like substance that she guessed must be some kind of preserving fluid.

'Yes!' cried the Doctor. 'Baseplate repetition filaments. If we move one down ...'

Carefully he extracted one of the frames, the sticky fluid oozing over his fingers.

Donna grimaced. 'Is that stuff dangerous?'

'Nah,' said the Doctor confidently, and then he frowned. 'Don't think so.'

To her horror, he raised the panel to his mouth and licked it. 'No,' he confirmed, but a moment later his eyes bulged and he clawed at his throat, making a hideous choking sound. She stepped forward to help him, but then his face cleared. He straightened up and grinned. 'No,' he said again.

'Oi!' she barked, more annoyed than amused.

Instead of apologising, the Doctor turned back to the rack, where he moved the panel a few rows down and snapped it into place.

'As I was saying, if we move one of these filaments down and then clip it into the foldback...' He glanced at Donna, indicating the panel with gooey fingers. 'Can you do that? Take all the rectangles, move them down to there?'

She nodded, but added huffily, 'And what does that do?'

'The ship's on neutral. For some reason, it's just idling. We need to get it back on full power.'

Without further explanation, he turned and strode towards the door.

'Hey, don't leave me on my own!' she shouted.

He paused, turned back. 'Donna, there is no one else on board this ship.'

'Hostile Action, remember?'

As if to underline her words, there came another *CLANG!* from somewhere beyond the room, in the vicinity of the main corridor.

'And what's that?' she said, alarmed.

He shrugged. 'A noise.'

'Oh, you're very helpful. Go on then. But hurry back, you little streak.'

He grinned, then turned and ducked out through the door.

His voice came floating back, echoing slightly. 'I need to find the spindle. That's not like wool. It's a water pivot.'

Good luck with that, Donna thought, and turned to the rack. Grimacing as the honey-like goo trickled over her fingers, she extracted the first panel.

As the Doctor had thought, the Spindle Room lay at the end of the left-hand corridor. This was an even smaller room than the flight deck and the Filament Room, crammed from floor to ceiling with what appeared to be myriad glass sculptures composed of complex tangles of transparent pipes through which bubbling water flowed. Each of these 'sculptures' was interconnected, in addition to which the pipes themselves were studded with adjustable valves, which meant that the system could be manually adapted, depending on the ship's requirements.

'Found it!' the Doctor yelled, strolling among the pipes and admiring the technology. 'Can you still hear me?'

Donna's voice came floating back. 'No.'

He chuckled to himself. 'Good, good! Won't be long!'

Reaching out, he twisted a valve and altered a pipe by a couple of millimetres. Immediately the bubbling of water became more intense, and the previously subliminal hum of energy from the ship became higher-pitched, a little more urgent.

The Doctor looked up, delighted. There was nothing wrong with the ship's engines, at any rate. And it was nice to be doing something constructive, even if their ultimate goal, at this point, seemed well-nigh unreachable.

Becoming engrossed in his task, he made a minute adjustment to another glass pipe.

In the Filament Room, Donna was enjoying the repetitive nature of the task. At first, she'd found the little plastic panels fiddly to extract, and the sticky gloop that adhered to her fingers made her feel queasy. But after a while she'd got into a rhythm with the panels, and had become so used to the gloop that it didn't bother her any more. She also found that concentrating on the simple task was helping to alleviate her anxiety, to the point that she had now entered an almost trance-like state. It was only the unexpected appearance of her own breath, emerging as a cloud of white vapour from her mouth, that snapped her from her reverie.

As the cloud dissipated, the Doctor entered the room and dropped onto his haunches beside her, bony knees sticking up. Silently he watched her working.

Donna glanced at him. 'Did it just get cold?'

'I think so,' he said.

She looked at him again. He seemed calm, but oddly intent. Assuming he'd simply finished his bit, and was now waiting for her to finish hers, she carried on moving the panels. After thirty seconds or so, she said quietly, 'I was thinking... and let me finish, because okay, I know I sound daft, but... I wonder how long they'll wait. Rose and Shaun and my mother. Standing there, in that alley. Waiting for the TARDIS to come back.' She felt emotion rising up and swallowed it down, and then she whispered, 'What if we never do?'

She expected him to reply, to offer reassuring words, but he didn't. Looking at him again, to gauge the expression on his face, she was surprised to see that he was just staring at her.

Intently.

The Doctor was still at work in the Spindle Room.

Still making minute adjustments to the myriad pipes. Still listening, nodding, occasionally giving a little 'hmm' of satisfaction.

All at once he shivered, as though an icy breeze had passed over him. He exhaled and saw the ghostly vapour of his breath hanging on the air. He was half-aware of Donna entering the room, kneeling beside him. Silently she watched him.

'It's getting cold,' he said. 'I hope I haven't turned the heating off by mistake. You were fast!'

'I did what you said,' she replied. She sounded dull, listless.

Stress catching up with her, the Doctor thought. *Making her tired.*

'Give me a minute,' he said. 'Got to get exactly the right millilitre.'

She said nothing. Just watched him.

The Doctor must be in one of his moods. *Moody spaceman*, Donna thought. Or maybe he was just making plans, pondering possible solutions, in that giant, supercharged brain of his.

If so, tough. Because she didn't like silence. And she especially didn't like the way her worries kept going round and round in her head. She needed to get them out, give voice to them.

And so, as she worked, moving the sticky panels from one slot to another, she prattled on, more for her benefit than his.

'I mean, they'll go home in the end. There's the house to sort out and everything. But they'll come back, the next day, and the next, and the next. And then… time will pass. Rose will grow up. She'll have a life. She might go back to that alley, once a year, for old times' sake, but she'll move on. Not Shaun, though. He'll keep going back, every single day. He's nice, you know, he's lovely. I hope you get to know him.'

'I hope so too,' the Doctor said, though he sounded distracted. 'And Wilf. Your grandfather. What would he do?'

She smiled fondly. 'Oh, him! He'd install himself with a sleeping bag and a thermos. He'd sit there for ever. Calling you every name under the sun. Wouldn't he?'

She expected the Doctor to smile in response, but he didn't. In that same distracted voice, he said, 'He's lovely, Wilf. Such a nice man. I'd love to see him again.'

In the Spindle Room, the Doctor was saying, 'It's funny, cos… I wonder where the TARDIS goes. At random. Maybe it lands on some outcrop, by the sea. And there's a tribe. And they worship it for a hundred years. Then they grow up and try to burn it. Then they get wise and preserve it.'

His eyes flickered from the glass pipes to Donna, who was still kneeling beside him. He half-expected her to riff along with him, throwing in dafter and dafter suggestions – the TARDIS meeting up with a bunch of other time machines, getting married, starting a little trans-dimensional family...

But she just knelt there. Her face expressionless. Watching him work.

Tired, he thought again.

Shrugging, he continued. 'Then they build a city, all around it, till the TARDIS is just a tiny little dot surrounded by skyscrapers and monorails. Then time passes and the city falls. It all gets swept away. And there's the TARDIS. Still on its outcrop. By the sea.'

He sighed. His flight of fancy had seemed amusing at first, but now it just seemed sad.

Quietly he said, 'She's the only thing I've got left.'

You've got me, he expected Donna to protest. But she didn't. Instead, quietly she asked, 'Do you miss home? Gallifrey.'

She spoke the word oddly. As though she'd snatched it from the air. Or dredged it up from somewhere deep.

The Doctor looked at her appraisingly. 'I suppose. I mean, yes, but... that got complicated.' He shook off his memories, and its attendant emotions, like a coat. 'And it's the least of our problems right now.'

Donna's stomach rumbled. She said, 'Do you think they've got a kitchen in this place? Do they have food?'

'My arms are too long,' said the Doctor.

Donna stopped working for a moment. Blinked. What?

The Doctor was an oddball. That was a given. He did and said unpredictable things sometimes. But that was just... *weird*.

She decided to let it go. 'Yeah, well... I skipped dinner last night. Because of you and the Meep.'

She expected him to pick up on what she'd said and start talking about the cute, furry little alien who'd turned out to be a raving psychopath. Instead, as if only realising it for the first time, he said, 'Oh, we get hungry, don't we?'

Donna looked at him. Was he taking the mick? He looked serious enough, though. And his unwavering gaze was starting to unsettle her.

'... Yeah,' she said slowly.

* * *

Puzzled, the Doctor tapped at a glass pipe.

'Strange. The system should be swimming by now. Those rectangles, did you move *all* of them down?'

'My arms are too long,' Donna said.

The Doctor couldn't really see why that should be a problem, but he decided to be encouraging. 'Yeah, I suppose it is a bit fiddly. Could you pop back and finish it?'

'My arms are too long,' she said again.

The Doctor frowned and turned his attention from the bubbling glass pipes. Donna's face – oddly serene, if slightly dazed-looking – was only inches from his own. 'OK,' he said. 'Are you all right?'

She gave him a quizzical 'haven't I already explained the problem?' look, and then, for the third time, she said, 'My arms are too long. Look.'

She lifted up an arm, and the Doctor staggered back, shocked. Donna was right. Her arms *were* too long. The one she had raised was maybe twice as long as it should have been and, right in front of his eyes, it was getting longer. Not only that, but her sleeves were getting longer too. Impossible as it seemed, her clothing was expanding along with her flesh. There was no ripping of skin, though, no cracking of bones, no straining of sinews. And Donna was clearly not in pain. She merely seemed a little nonplussed, as if what was happening to her body was no more than a minor inconvenience.

Her arms grew longer still, and as they lengthened, they also thickened, the limbs becoming as thick as tree trunks, the hands on the end of them swelling. When the palm of the hand she was holding up was as big as a tea tray and the fingers as long as rolling pins, it clumped to the floor, as if too heavy to lift.

The Doctor's mind raced. What was happening here? Possible explanations occurred to him – alien virus, dimensional anomaly, corrupted DNA stabiliser – but none seemed quite to fit the bill. For Donna's sake, he knew the most important thing was to stay calm, though she seemed calm enough herself, which was strange – unless she was in shock.

'It's okay,' he said, 'I've got you. Whatever this is, we can...'

His voice trailed off. She had cocked her head to one side, and was now regarding him with cold curiosity, as if he was some rare and interesting specimen.

And now a new possibility occurred to him. A far more worrying one.

'Are you even Donna?' he asked her.

* * *

In the Filament Room, Donna was still doggedly working away. But she felt wary now, unsettled by the presence of the Doctor, who was just crouching there on the floor, staring at her.

Suddenly, from a distance, a voice called to her. The Doctor's voice.

'Donna? Donna, are you there?'

Donna jumped, as though someone had sneaked up behind her and put a hand on her shoulder. She looked again at the Doctor, who was still crouching, motionless, eyes unblinking.

'How are you doing that?' she said.

But then, his knees unbending slowly, he stood up, and any further words dried in her throat. Because as he rose to his feet, the Doctor's hands stayed where they were, resting on the floor, his arms extending, stretching like toffee; his sleeves too. And glancing down, Donna saw that his hands were now *huge*, twice as big as his head, the hands of a giant.

With a sense of mild regret, the Doctor said, 'I don't know why, but the arms are so very difficult.'

And then, his face still expressionless, he lurched towards her.

Gilvane

Donna backed away, so freaked out by the grotesque sight she felt as though beetles were scuttling all over her.

The Doctor's voice came again from afar, a little more urgent this time. 'Donna? Are you there?'

It gave her the courage she needed. The courage to leap past the creepy Doctor with the overlong arms and the gigantic hands, and out into the corridor.

The distance to the three-way intersection was not long, no more than a dozen steps, but Donna knew all too well that when you had a monstrous thing behind you, each step could seem like a mile. She was relieved when the Doctor – the *real* Doctor – burst from the room at the opposite end of the corridor and began running towards her, heading for the intersection from his end.

Her joy quickly changed to horror, though, when another figure emerged from the room behind him.

Oh my God, she thought, *that's me!*

It *was* her. Down to the smallest detail – face, hair, red and pink jumper.

Except... this version of her had hideously long arms. And attached to the ends of them were hands that looked as big and heavy as anvils. Grotesquely, this version of herself was pursuing the Doctor – the real Doctor – by *throwing* the hands ahead of her body, as if they were a pair of anchors on a chain, then pulling herself forward, overtaking the hands, and yanking on them hard enough to swing them forward again.

All of this Donna registered in the few seconds it took to run the length of the corridor and meet the Doctor at the intersection. They clutched at one another, as though needing the contact, the reassurance. Then Donna saw the look of fascinated horror on the real Doctor's face as he glanced over her shoulder, and twisted round. She saw that the second Doctor, the Doctor-copy, was about halfway down the corridor. Bizarrely, he was leaning forward, dragging his huge hands on the floor behind him, as though they were a pair of heavily laden sleighs.

'What are they?' she yelled.

'They're us!' the Doctor yelled back.

Donna was appalled at the idea. 'They're *not* us!'

Still hauling his massive hands, the Doctor-copy, his voice strained with effort, spoke up. 'The notion … of shape … is strange.'

The Donna-copy, halfway down the opposite corridor, replied, 'It limits. It is limiting.'

The Doctor swivelled, looking from the Doctor-copy to the Donna-copy. 'OK,' he called, raising his hands placatingly. 'Whatever shape you want to take, that's fine. You can do whatever you want. I just want to say, it's very nice to meet you. I'm the Doctor, this is Donna.'

'So are they,' Donna muttered.

Despite the Doctor's efforts, the copies continued their remorseless advance, their faces set, eyes cold.

The Doctor tapped Donna on the shoulder, and together they began backing down the tunnel that led to the automatic door into the main corridor. Even now, the Doctor refused to give up his attempt to get through to the copies.

'If you can just get those bodies to calm down,' he said, 'we can talk. That'll be nice. Don't you think?'

Slowly but surely, the copies kept coming.

Donna said nervously, 'They're looking at us like food.'

Latching on to her words, the Doctor-copy said, 'Food is interesting. Because once I sort out the arms …' He stopped, a look of concentration on his face. And slowly the arms began to reel in, and the hands started to shrink, returning to normal. '… then I have a problem with the jaw.'

Abruptly, horrifically, the Doctor-copy's jaw dropped. Donna thought of all those different versions of *A Christmas Carol* she'd seen over the years. As a kid, she'd always dreaded the bit where the ghost of Jacob Marley unties the binding around his chin and his jaw drops open like a faulty portcullis.

This was like that, but worse. Firstly, because it was happening to a thing that looked like the Doctor. And secondly, because it was happening here, right in front of her.

The Doctor-copy's cheeks didn't split or tear as his jaw dropped. The skin simply stretched like elastic, as the jaw dropped, first to his chest, and then even lower, right down to his belly button.

Donna felt sick. And it didn't help matters when the Doctor-copy cradled the swinging jaw in his interlocked hands, then casually rammed it back into place with a wet, suction-like sound – *schlup!*

From the opposite corridor, the Donna-copy said, 'It's the knees. How many knees?'

'Two,' said the Doctor-copy.

'Two in total or two on each leg?'

Donna looked back at her double, and saw that not only was her right leg now twice as long as it should be, but that it was jointed in two places, resembling a lopsided N. The two knees tilted and swayed like opposite ends of a see-saw, causing the Donna-copy to move awkwardly, with a rolling lurch, like an injured crab.

Still backing slowly towards the automatic door into the main corridor, the Doctor asked, 'Where did you come from? You're not part of this ship, are you? Did you come from outside?'

'We came from the nothing,' said the Donna-copy.

'We are not-things,' added the Doctor-copy.

'But *you* are not nothing,' the Donna-copy observed with relish.

'No,' the Doctor agreed. 'I think you'll find we're quite something!'

So saying, he grabbed Donna by the hand and together they turned and raced for the automatic door. For a horrible moment Donna felt certain it wouldn't open. But, to her immense relief, the door slid smoothly aside at their approach.

She and the Doctor ran out into the main corridor and leaped into the hover-buggy, which was still waiting patiently where they had left it. The Doctor took the driving seat again. Like a practised stunt driver, he spun the hover-buggy around on its cushion of air, and a second later they were zipping down the corridor so swiftly that Donna felt as if she was in a wind tunnel, her hair streaming in her wake like a flag.

The whoosh of air in her ears didn't prevent her from hearing the echoing thuds behind them, though. She twisted in her seat to see the copies bearing down on them.

To her horror they had transformed again, this time into huge gorilla-like beasts, their massive hands on the ends of their overlong arms thudding into the floor like jackhammers as they propelled themselves along.

'Doctor!' Donna warned.

He glanced over his shoulder. 'What the …?'

The copies were still growing, their legs lengthening, shoulders bulking, heads elongating, features stretching. They all but filled the vast corridor now, two colossal, nightmarish creatures, galumphing along in their pursuit of the hover-buggy. Clumsy and heavy they may have been, but their sheer size meant they were gaining on their prey with each lumbering step.

The Doctor and Donna faced front again, leaning forwards as if that would help.

'*Come on!*' the Doctor yelled at the hover-buggy, yanking on the gear-stick and pressing the accelerator down as hard as he could.

'Go faster!' screamed Donna.

'I'm *trying!*' the Doctor bellowed back.

But instead of accelerating, the hover-buggy actually seemed to be slowing down. Frantically the Doctor manipulated the simple controls, trying to work out what was wrong.

'Why's it … what's it … *what?*' he spluttered.

He and Donna twisted in unison, and saw that the Doctor-copy, vast and monstrous, was now looming over them like a hideously misshapen inflatable. He had grabbed hold of the back of the buggy with his gigantic excavator-scoop of a hand, but although he was managing to slow the buggy down, he still didn't have a strong enough grip to stop their progress completely.

'Oh no, you don't!' yelled Donna, yanking at one of the metal poles that supported the flimsy vehicle's overhead canopy.

To her surprise, the pole snapped off in her hands with barely any resistance. She was pleased to note that it felt sturdy enough to use as a weapon, though. And so, twisting round further in her seat, she started to batter at the Doctor-copy's giant hand.

The Doctor, meanwhile, was struggling at the wheel, the hover-buggy thrashing from side to side, like a fish struggling to free itself from an angler's hook.

'*I can't control it!*' he yelled.

Beside him, facing backwards, Donna continued to batter at the Doctor-copy's hand. She concentrated on the fingers that were clinging to the back of the buggy, but couldn't get them to relinquish their grip. She took a quick breath, then redoubled her efforts.

'You! Stupid! Big! Hand!' she yelled, punctuating each word with a fresh whack from the pole.

Finally, she did it. As if the blow had landed in a particularly sensitive area, the fingers suddenly sprang apart. Donna's whoop of triumph was short-lived because, as the hover-buggy leaped forward, it also went horribly out of control, like a small child running full-tilt down a steep hill. It veered and swung, and then, despite the Doctor's efforts, went careering towards the right-hand wall.

'*No-no-no-no-no!*' he cried, while Donna covered her face and yelled, '*Whooooa!*'

The hover-buggy slammed into one of the metal stanchions, rupturing it, causing a jet of super-pressured steam to shoot out in a hissing *whoosh!*

Rebounding off the stanchion, the hover-buggy spun round, then hit the opposite wall of the corridor side on, metal scraping against metal with such force that sparks flew up in an arcing shower.

The buggy had lost enough momentum now for the Donna-copy, outpacing her finger-stung companion, to have caught them up. She lashed out like a cat batting at a fleeing mouse, and swiped the rear end of the buggy as it bounced off the wall. The blow sent the buggy spinning like a top. Still moving forward, though haphazardly now, it bounced along the floor like a flat stone skimming across the surface of a lake, each jarring impact sending a profusion of white-hot sparks erupting into the air.

Throughout this, the Doctor kept wrenching on the steering wheel, twisting it this way and that, trying to bring the stricken vehicle under control. The buggy, though, had never been designed for such rough treatment and, in the end, the wheel simply snapped off in his hand.

He goggled at it almost comically, then tossed it aside. All the Doctor and Donna could do now was hang on while the hover-buggy continued to spin. Feeling sick and dizzy, Donna was torn between wanting to escape their monstrous pursuers and wishing the buggy would stop so that she could get off. She closed her eyes and only opened them again when she realised the buggy was slowing down.

It took her a moment to get her bearings. Although the buggy had stopped spinning, it was still, for the moment, moving along the corridor – but it was going backwards. Donna's vision was now filled with the terrifying sight of the Doctor-copy and the Donna-copy surging towards them. The creatures had grown to such monstrous proportions that their combined bulk almost completely filled the vast, wide corridor. They were squeezed together as they continued to advance, a remorselessly rolling avalanche of flesh and clothing, in which huge, flopping hands, limbs like immense pistons, and snarling, contorted features could occasionally be seen.

As the buggy – still scraping backwards along the floor, still throwing up the occasional shower of sparks – continued to slow, so the mountainous abomination of juddering, twisting, writhing flesh continued to gain on them. The creatures were now no more than ten metres away... now eight... now six.

By the time the buggy finally scraped to a halt, the fleshy monstrosities were only five metres behind them, and all set to crush, or absorb, or consume them...

And then, with a shuddering jerk, they stopped.

Donna's immediate thought was that the things had only come to a halt because they knew the pursuit was over and were relishing the moment before they pounced. Then, gradually, it dawned on her that that wasn't the case. The creatures had stopped because they were *wedged*. Stuck fast. They had swelled to such an extent that they had filled the corridor as effectively as expanding foam in a wall cavity.

Relieved as she was, she was also sickened at the sight of all that warped and twisted flesh. The two faces, pressed together, looked like the reflections of faces in a funhouse mirror: one of the Doctor-copy's eyes vast and bulging, as if about to pop; the Donna-copy's mouth a zigzagging red line, like a child's drawing of a staircase. And jumbled in between the faces were limbs and joints and fingers, all of them twitching and shifting. As Donna stepped from one side of the damaged buggy and the Doctor stepped from the other, the Doctor-copy's massively swollen eye blinked once, then swivelled to regard them.

'What are they?' Donna asked, breathless.

Before the Doctor could reply, there was a crumping bang from the engine of the buggy, and then, in a puff of thick, greasy smoke, the little vehicle simply collapsed in upon itself.

The Doctor gave it a little nod of acknowledgement, as though thanking it for its loyal service and noble sacrifice, then he began to walk towards the wall of flesh.

'Oh no, don't,' Donna said, hanging back.

The Doctor paused, glanced over his shoulder. 'We've got to see.'

He advanced again, stopping only a metre or so from the vast eye. It watched him as a god might watch the approach of an insect.

'It's strange enough, my face coming back,' he mused. 'But not this big.'

Donna still couldn't bring herself to get closer to the thing. Not only was it skin-crawlingly nightmarish, but she was nervous that something would lash out from it – a tongue, or a finger, or even some sort of flesh tentacle that would wrap around the Doctor and drag him in.

She tried to make herself think constructively, logically, like the Doctor always did. 'The airlock door. Three years ago. That's when they got in.'

To her horror, the Doctor leaned in even closer to the eye. For a moment she thought he was going to poke it, or even lick it. But then he dropped back on to his heels and said, 'No-things. No control of shape. No *concept* of shape. Or size.'

Still trying to think logically, scientifically, Donna said, 'How can they get bigger? Cos you only have a certain amount of mass, don't you? Shaun used to complain about that, watching

Venom films. He'd say where does the extra mass come from?'

The Doctor gave no immediate answer. 'It got colder,' he murmured eventually.

'Oh. It got colder for me, yeah.'

'Heat into mass? But they're not just physical copies, they've got our thoughts too. That other Donna mentioned Gallifrey.'

'The other Doctor said Wilf.'

'They've got our memories,' the Doctor said, gazing into the eye as though he might be able to see right through it, into the mind of the thing itself.

'OK,' said Donna. 'So, they're copies, with memories and mass. But what I don't get is … why do they hate us?'

The wall of flesh suddenly shifted. Not just a twitch this time, but a significant movement, resulting in one of the Donna-copy's massive hands thumping out on to the floor. It lay there, palm up, fingers twitching. The size of a Range Rover.

'That's my hand,' said Donna with a sense of wonder and disbelief.

The flesh mountain flexed, then shifted again. And looking up, the Doctor saw that it was no longer jammed right up against the roof. There was a gap there now. There was wriggle-room.

'They're getting free,' he warned.

He began to back off; Donna too, even though she was already a few metres behind him. Their eyes flickered across the jumble of body parts, which were more active now, as they tried to untangle themselves.

'We should reason with them,' the Doctor said, ever the diplomat. 'Make peace. Welcome them to our side of the universe.'

As the flesh mountain convulsed, the Doctor-copy's contorted mouth opened and unleashed a bestial, snarling roar.

'Maybe later,' amended the Doctor. Then he and Donna turned and ran.

Behind them, the flesh mountain convulsed again, bits of it flopping forward, breaking free. Now the Donna-copy's zigzagging mouth opened, and she released an ululating wail.

To Donna, it sounded like an attack cry.

She and the Doctor ran past the still-smoking ruin of the hover-buggy, the Doctor frantically scanning the walls.

'I know, I know, I know,' he was muttering, and then he suddenly pointed and shouted, 'Ladder!'

It was hardly a ladder, more a series of vertical, semicircular rungs embedded in the curving metal wall. Donna had no idea whether the rungs were functional or merely a design feature, but at this moment she didn't really care. The important thing was that they led to an opening, a conduit of some sort, high above her head, near the ceiling.

Climbing all the way up there was a daunting prospect. Just craning her neck to look up made Donna feel dizzy.

'Do you think? Maybe up there?' the Doctor ventured. His face said: *I know this is a rubbish plan, but it's the only one I've got.*

There was a renewed screech of rage, coordinated this time, from the mouths of the creatures, and the barricade of flesh shifted again, gaps opening not only beneath the roof, but also around the sides.

'Let's go!' Donna said, running towards the wall, but the Doctor was already ahead of her. As he scuttled up the rungs like a monkey, she threw herself at the wall in his wake. Climbing after him, Donna tried not to think of the consequences should they fall, or should the shapeshifters catch up with them.

Two minutes later, they were making good progress, were perhaps a third of the way to the conduit they were aiming for, when the mechanical voice they had heard twice before boomed from the hidden speakers again.

'*Brate,*' it said.

'Oh, not now!' yelled the Doctor, as the walls once more began to move, panels clicking, sliding, flipping, just as before.

Terrified, Donna clung on, wondering what would happen if her hand and foot holds suddenly disappeared. She'd fall to the floor, and from this height she'd almost certainly break bones, or worse.

Luckily for her, the rungs she was clinging to didn't disappear. But *un*luckily, the whole section of wall she was on suddenly began to slide sideways, taking her back *towards* the convulsing wall of flesh.

She wailed in despair: '*Doctor!*'

Stond

The Doctor could only look on helplessly as Donna was carried away from him. It was like being a shipwreck survivor, clinging to the side of a rescue ship and seeing the friend below you swept away by a surging wave.

Although he knew it was hopeless, he reached out towards her, shouting, 'It's okay, I'm right here!'

But suddenly he wasn't. The section of wall he was on spun 180 degrees, like a secret panel in a country house, and he was plunged into darkness.

No, not darkness. It had only seemed so at first, because the place he had left had been so white and well lit.

As the panel clicked into place, the Doctor found himself in a dark and dingy service duct, which he knew must run parallel to the main corridor. It was composed of metre-long sections of hexagonal piping made of dark grey metal, the fixings between each section like a thick metal collar through which he'd have to duck. The walls here were dirty and oil-streaked, and there was barely enough room for him to stand up. Fortunately, the conduit was lit, but only dimly, by inset spotlights that emitted a sickly green glow.

Stepping down from his perch halfway up the wall into the conduit itself, he shoved at the section of wall, hoping it would flip back round again. It didn't surprise him to discover, however, that it was now locked firmly into place.

'Donna?' he shouted. 'Donna! Donna!'

His voice boomed around him, echoing off the walls, but there was no reply.

Donna was still clamped to the wall, still rushing sideways, towards the mountain of flesh. Just when it seemed she would have to make the choice between colliding with the fleshy barricade or leaping off and taking her chances with the floor below, the section of wall to which she clung came to a halt with a hefty *chunk!* Next moment there was a medley of ratcheting clicks, as though a thousand locks were springing open all at once. She waited, breathless with apprehension – and then her worst fears were confirmed. The projecting rungs, up which she'd been climbing, withdrew smoothly into the wall, leaving her with no hand or foot holds.

Before she could plummet to her death, however, her section of wall tilted back, like the lid of a flip-top bin, the more acute angle causing her not to fall from the curving wall, but to slide down it. Assuming she'd hit the floor at some speed but not with the kind of impact to break bones, she prepared herself to roll, jump to her feet, and run.

But the ship's latest reconfiguration program had one more surprise in store. As she neared the floor, she was horrified to see the section she was aiming for sliding back like a trap door.

With a scream, she disappeared into the square hole in the floor. For what seemed an eternity, she continued to slide through darkness. Although it was terrifying, she was slightly consoled by the fact that, rather than picking up speed as she descended, she was actually slowing down. She realised the slide must be levelling out, becoming flatter – and then she was unceremoniously spat out onto a hard metal floor, landing with a jarring impact on her right hip and elbow.

She lay for a few moments, her ears ringing, peripherally aware of the far-off ticking and clicking, which was now slowing down. When it had stopped completely, she rose, groaning, to a sitting position and looked around.

She was in a narrow, hexagonal tunnel, illuminated by dim, reddish lights set into the ceiling. Although grateful to have escaped the pursuing shapeshifters – for now at least – she was suddenly overwhelmed by a feeling she hadn't experienced for a long time, not since she had last travelled with the Doctor.

It was the feeling of being cut off, stranded, and a long, long way from home.

Moving through his own section of piping in a half-crouch, the Doctor stopped every few metres to bang on the walls and shout.

'Donna! Are you there? Donna!' He listened, but so far had received no reply. Regardless, he yelled, 'I'll find you! I *will* find you! Don't move! Stay where you are!'

Although each section of pipe looked the same, the Doctor knew from experience and logic that eventually he'd find something new, something different. Sure enough, after a further few minutes of trudging, he did.

It was another ladder. Or at least, another set of rungs affixed to the wall, this time leading down through a gap in the floor. Dropping to his knees, he peered into the shaft, but all he could see was blackness.

Undaunted, he grabbed hold of the rungs and began to descend.

Rising painfully to her feet, Donna peered up the shaft she had been dumped out of, but all she could see was blackness.

'I came down!' she yelled. 'About two floors! Depending how big a floor is!'

Then she realised what she was doing and murmured ruefully, 'And if I keep shouting, they'll hear me. I'll head back up, yeah?'

Only silence greeted her words.

'Yeah,' she answered herself.

The Doctor descended only a couple of levels before stepping off the ladder. He could have kept going, but knew any choice was pot luck. Who knew how the ship's inner workings were arranged, and what bits led to where?

He decided to stroll along here for a bit, see what was what. If he didn't find anything, he could always descend to another level.

As he moved off to the right – another random choice – he muttered, 'Fenslaw. Collis. Brate.'

What did those words mean?

Mentally he started to break them down,

reconstruct them, look at them from all angles. It would give him something to do while he searched for Donna.

Clang!

Donna stopped with a gasp, her shoulders hunching instinctively. That sound again! What was it? It was faint this time, distant, coming to her through god-knew-how-many layers of metal.

She looked up at the ceiling, only a few inches above her head, and experienced a sudden prickling of claustrophobia.

No. She wouldn't give in to irrational fears. She would do what the Doctor always did – keep moving forward, keep looking for a way out.

She started walking again, her footsteps echoing in the dimly lit conduit. *Clung-clung, clung-clung, clung-clung*... like tiny versions of the metallic clang she'd heard moments ago.

Despite her resolve, Donna couldn't shake off the feeling she was being followed. She glanced back, but the lighting in the pipe was so dim that after just a few metres the space behind her faded into a clotted mass of red-tinged shadow.

She kept walking – *clung-clung, clung-clung, clung-clung*...

Were they only echoes, or was another set of footsteps matching hers?

She came to an abrupt halt and listened. To her horror, the footsteps behind her continued. But only for a couple of steps, before they stopped. She looked behind her again.

Nothing but swirling shadow.

Fighting the urge to panic, to run, she took another half-dozen steps forward – *clung-clung, clung-clung, clung-clung* – then stopped.

The footsteps continued – one, two – then stopped.

Silence.

Donna's mouth was dry. She turned and stared hard into the reddish mass behind her.

Was there something there? The suggestion of movement?

Keep going, she thought, *keep going*.

She turned away…

SCHUNK!

A sound like a guillotine falling, no more than a metre behind her.

She spun, heart leaping, pulse hammering in her throat, all her nerve endings fizzing with shock…

…and *oh no, oh no*, there was the Donna-copy, right behind her.

Donna staggered back – and the Donna-copy staggered back too, an identical movement.

Was it mocking her? Deliberately replicating her actions? But it had staggered back at exactly the same moment she had. So how could it know...? And then she realised.

She laughed. A hollow sound, almost a sob, full of relief.

What she was looking at, the other her – it wasn't the Donna-copy, it was her own reflection. The guillotine-sound had been caused by a mirrored barrier sliding out or down, blocking her way back.

This place! She took deep breaths, leaning forward with her hands on her knees. Then she straightened up. If nothing else, the barrier had made the decision for her. There was only one way she could go now.

She turned and walked on.

The greenish lights around the Doctor dipped, began to flicker.

'Oh, don't,' he muttered, coming to a halt. He was fearful not of being plunged into darkness – though that would have been inconvenient – but of what the sudden power drain might indicate. Of who, or rather what, might be siphoning it off.

Aware that it had become suddenly and

unnaturally cold, he exhaled – and saw the white vapour of his breath hanging in the air before him.

Turning slowly in a circle, he peered into the gloom, and that was when he saw it. Inset into the metal wall about two metres away.

A door.

Donna stopped, shivered. Was she imagining it, or had it suddenly turned as cold as a freezer?

She breathed out, and was horrified to see a white cloud of steam jet from her mouth.

It must be in here with her. The creature. The thing. *Oh god, oh god…*

Frantically, she glanced behind her – and realised what she had walked past without noticing.

It was so flush with the wall it was almost invisible, but it was definitely there.

The outline of a door.

It was hard to tell what the room had once been used for. It was octagonal in shape, and five of its walls were dominated by large windows, which offered a panoramic view of the blackness outside. Of the three windowless walls, two were inset with metal doors, while the remaining wall, in the middle of these, was blank.

The layout was neat, pleasingly symmetrical. There was no equipment in the room. The floor was a white expanse.

All at once, the lights in the room began to flicker. One of the two doors opened, and then, almost immediately afterwards, the other. A figure stepped out of each.

From the left-hand door emerged the Doctor. From the right-hand door emerged Donna.

As the lights ceased flickering, and burned brightly again, each of them came to an abrupt halt, and stared at the other.

The room, illuminated by cold, blue lighting, was clearly a workshop of some kind. It was octagonal in shape, six of its walls partly obscured by random bits of equipment, many of which were in need of repair. The other two walls, those standing roughly north-east and north-west, had thick metal doors inset into them. The doors were scuffed and streaked with oil, as were the walls. It was silent in the room, and nothing moved – but suddenly the icy blue lights began to flicker.

Then, almost in unison, the two doors slid open. A figure stepped from each – the Doctor from the right-hand door, Donna from the left. Each of the figures came to a halt and stared at the other. Each looked hopeful, but also wary. Each looked as though they wanted to run to the other, and at the same time maintain the half-dozen metres of floor space between them.

After a moment's silence, the Doctor said, 'Is it…?'

Simultaneously Donna said, 'Are you…?'

They stopped. Then Donna sighed and said, 'Is that you?'

'But… it got cold,' the Doctor said warily.

'It got cold for me too,' replied Donna, and put a hand over her heart. 'Look, I'm me, I swear. I'm really, really me.'

'Well, so am I!' Then the Doctor shook his head. 'That's not going to work. Okay, tell me, how many hearts have I got?'

'Two,' she said without hesitation.

'Well then – it's me! No, hold on, that doesn't work either…'

In the empty room with all the windows, the other Doctor and Donna were keeping their distance too.

'No, but look,' Donna was saying, 'I can't stretch. My arm is not too long.' She held her arm out to demonstrate. 'I'm trying. That's all I've got.'

'But if you were them, you'd *pretend* that you couldn't stretch,' the Doctor pointed out.

She took a step forward, held her arm out towards him. 'Then pull my arm.'

The Doctor stayed where he was, scratched the back of his head. 'Yes, but … maybe that's what you want me to do.'

She rolled her eyes. 'What for?'

'I don't know!'

Donna jabbed a finger at him, and said triumphantly, 'Well, you're not the Doctor then, because he knows everything.'

'Except for the million times when I don't, and I tell you so – don't I?'

'OK,' she conceded, 'that's true. Except if I *know* that's true, then I'm me!'

The Doctor shrugged. 'Maybe we're both real.'

In the workshop, the Doctor's face suddenly brightened as he had an idea.

'Tell you what. Look! I'll take my tie off.' He yanked at the loose knot in his grey tie until it came free, then threw it to one side.

Donna eyed the tie, crumpled up on the floor like a shed snakeskin. 'What does that prove?'

'Well, they might have a different perception of

surface. Skin and clothes might be the same thing. So if we meet another Doctor, with his tie, that's not me.'

Donna grimaced, unconvinced. 'But you're just making all this up.'

'I always do,' he said.

They both laughed. But it was a small sound, and a little desperate.

She gave a shaky sigh. 'That *sounds* like you.'

'Sounds like you too,' said the Doctor. 'But that's the point, isn't it? You *would* sound like you.'

'OK,' she said, thinking. 'Where was I born?'

'You're from Chiswick,' said the Doctor in the empty room. 'I know that.'

'OK,' said Donna, and looked at him shrewdly. 'So where are *you* from?'

The Doctor frowned. 'No, but we've done that. We talked about that – back there, out loud. All four of us know it's Gallifrey.'

Quietly, almost kindly, she said, 'Except… it's not.'

His frown deepened. 'What do you mean?'

'You don't know where you're from.'

Looking flustered, the Doctor said, 'How do you know that? How does anyone know? How does Donna know?'

'Back on Earth,' she said, 'when I was the DoctorDonna, I saw your mind. I've had fifteen years without you, and I saw everything that's happened to you since. And, oh my god, it *hurt* …'

The Doctor's face creased. He backed up, as if trying to distance himself not just from her, but from the pain. His words were raw, bitter. 'If you're doing this … to break me down …'

'But we haven't stopped to talk,' she said. 'We haven't had a chance. It's always like that with you, running from one thing to the next. But … I saw it. In your head. The Flux.'

'It destroyed half the universe,' said the Doctor bitterly. 'Because of me. We stand here now, on the edge of creation – a creation which I devastated. So yes. I keep running. Of course I do. How am I supposed to look back at that?'

'It wasn't your fault,' said Donna gently.

His face twisted in anger. '*I know!*'

The air itself seemed momentarily shocked by the rawness of his despair.

Then, softly, cutting through the silence, Donna said, 'I'm sorry.'

The Doctor's head dropped, and he released a shuddering breath. When he met her eyes again, he looked haggard, and so, so lonely.

'Donna,' he said, and it was almost a plea. 'Is that you?'

'Yeah,' she said. 'And you're not alone. Cos we shared a mind.'

'You can't fake that,' he said, and a sad, weary smile broke across his face. 'All those years. I missed you.'

He all but ran across the room towards her, arms stretched wide for a hug. Donna took three steps towards him ... then her legs turned to gooey, colourless liquid beneath her.

Ratico

The Donna-copy kept moving forward, but she was sliding now, sinking down. Finally, unable to maintain her momentum, she came to a halt, a perfect representation of Donna from the waist up, but with a gooey, slimy, bubbling trail, like that left by a giant mollusc, stretching behind her.

The Doctor, who had already clumped to a stop, looked down at her, appalled.

The Donna-copy was clearly delighted to have fooled him. She was grinning from ear to ear.

'Ohhh *no!*' she exclaimed, as if she'd let slip a lovely surprise she'd been planning for him. 'I just couldn't keep it together. You are so *amazing!*'

The Doctor didn't feel amazing. On the contrary, he was so sickened by how he'd laid bare his emotions – exposed the vulnerabilities he usually fought so fiercely to maintain – to this ... *thing*, that he could barely speak.

'You ... you're ...' he spluttered.

'We stare at that universe, so far away,' the

Donna-copy said. 'But you have *owned* it! You are such a prize. *What are you?*'

The Doctor had no words. At that moment, he had nothing but disgust and hate inside him, much of it directed at himself. Unable to bear looking at the gleeful, dissolving Donna-copy any longer, he turned and fled.

'You were born in Chiswick,' the Doctor-copy said.

In the workshop, Donna was still trying to work out whether this was the real Doctor or not. She held up a finger.

'Ah! Well! No! Because! Strange little fact. I was born in Southampton.'

The Doctor-copy spread his hands, pulled a 'not-fair' face. 'Yes, but I didn't know that. Cos I never did. And if I didn't know … then that means I'm real!'

He looked triumphant. Donna thought about it.

'That makes sense,' she said eventually.

The Doctor-copy jabbed a finger at her. 'But is it you?'

Donna knew it was, but how to convince him? Taking a breath, she said, 'I was born in Southampton, cos Mum and Dad were there for the weekend, visiting Aunty Iris. My mother was nine months pregnant, but would Iris come to her? No, she would not. So I arrived. In Southampton. Which allowed my mother to say I was a problem from the day I was born – and I have not come to the edge of the universe to discover I'm still dealing with that. So, yes, you can copy my memory, but there's only one person who can understand my family like that, and that's me. I'm definitely Donna. Where's your tie?'

The Doctor-copy blinked at the unexpected question. 'What?'

Donna pointed at the now-empty floor, where his discarded tie had been lying. 'Your tie. Where's it gone?'

'I took it off,' he said, baffled.

'I know. It was there, on the floor. It was right there, and the walls haven't moved – so where is it?'

The Doctor-copy rolled his eyes playfully. 'Oh, I *seeee*. When something is gone, it keeps existing.'

He started to laugh. He laughed and laughed. He tilted his head back, guffawing at the ceiling.

Donna watched in horror as the Doctor-copy *continued* to tilt his head back. He tilted it back further than it was supposed to go, and then further still. His neck stretched to accommodate the movement. His back arched like a bow, his neck extending like the thick, tensile body of a snake, until his head was touching the floor.

But even then, he didn't stop. His head dipped back further, continuing the arc, so that his face came parallel with the floor, his nose almost brushing it. Then it stretched further still, until his face rose up from the floor, and he was staring at Donna from between his own feet.

He grinned at her. The grin was far too wide.

'Aunty Iris, Mummy and Daddy, yap yap yap,' he scoffed. 'Why does he travel with someone as *stupid* as *you?*'

Then, his body horribly contorted, his grinning face glaring at her from between his own knees, the Doctor-copy scuttled towards her like a huge, misshapen scorpion.

Donna ran.

The Doctor was running back through the service duct; running wildly, stumbling and ricocheting off the metal walls, his head spinning, raging.

Everything that the Donna-copy had said to him was crashing and exploding in his mind. All the destruction he'd caused, the lives he'd ruined. All the death and heartache that had happened because of him.

And he'd thought she was Donna! He thought he'd been unburdening himself to someone who understood and cared. Someone who'd shared his mind, and knew how much guilt and grief and regret was stored up in there.

He staggered to a halt. He had to let it out. All the rage, all the anguish.

Turning, he punched the walls, again and again, frenziedly, madly, letting it all go.

And as he punched, he screamed, yelled, the sound echoing around him, a mad, furious ululation. He punched until his fists were numb, and he screamed until his throat was sore.

And then he stopped. Began to rebuild himself.

He straightened up; pulled back his shoulders; clenched and unclenched his tingling, bruised fists.

He swallowed, sniffed.

And he summoned it from deep within himself – that iron resolve, that timeless strength, that determination to do the best he possibly could. That *armour*.

'Good,' he said.

And he moved on.

A long way from the conflict at the far end of the ship, unseen and all but forgotten, the little robot, which Donna had christened Jimbo, was once again on the move.

With a clank and a hiss, it took one more slow, deliberate step forward. Then it halted once again.

Donna was moving back through the service duct as fast as she could, her breath rasping in her throat. She looked constantly behind her, each moment expecting the horribly contorted Doctor-copy to loom grinning out of the shadows.

One thing preyed on her mind: the mirrored barrier. If it was still there, blocking her way, she'd be trapped.

Maybe it knows that, she thought. *Maybe that's why it's not followed me yet. It knows it can take its—*

'Gilvane.'

The robotic voice, booming from hidden speakers, made her jump out of her skin. Even as the echoes of it were bouncing around the metallic walls of the pipe, Donna heard the familiar click-click-clicking, signalling the start of another realignment.

'Oh no,' she said as the lights began to flicker. She stood, braced, eyes darting everywhere, every moment expecting the ceiling to fall and crush her, or the floor to disappear, or the walls to slam together with her stuck between them.

* * *

The Doctor stood calmly as the lights flickered and the wall panels shifted around him. He concentrated, zoned in, his eyes following the patterns. If he was right ... and he was! To his left, a recess was forming – a corridor. And at the end of the corridor ...

A door.

The sound and movement around her made Donna feel she was standing amongst a cloud of metallic butterflies. If she could shake off the fear of being an organic creature caught inside a vast machine with a million moving parts, she could almost view it as a soothing experience.

At least the floor and ceiling were still solid – for now, at least. She watched the panels on the right-hand wall slide sideways, sink back, overlap one another. It was mesmeric, and it seemed almost as though she could step forward, into the wall ...

And then she realised. She *could* step forward into the wall. Because a corridor was forming. And at the end of the corridor ...

A door.

The room was large, low-ceilinged, a door in every corner, as if it needed to be accessed from multiple directions. It was an industrial room, full of copper-coloured barrels and cylinders in a myriad shapes and sizes, all of which were linked together in a convoluted arrangement. Above the click-click-clicking of reconfiguration, which was affecting two of the walls, the room was full of the throb of engines and the rushing of water, as if it was located close to the heart of the ship's workings. It was the kind of room where you might expect to find sweaty, grimy workers toiling away. But like the rest of the ship, it was empty.

Until...

With the lights in the room flickering, a door in one of the walls suddenly slid open, and the Doctor – or *a* Doctor – stepped through it.

The click-click-clicking abruptly stopped, the walls settling back into solidity, as a door in the bottom right-hand corner opened, and a Donna rushed into the room.

Next, two doors opened simultaneously – bottom left and top right – and a second Doctor, followed by a second Donna, appeared.

The lights stopped flickering, and now all four entrants – two Doctors, two Donnas – could see one another clearly. The Doctors were wearing identical ties, and all four of the arrivals looked at the others with wary, fearful expressions.

The Donna who had just entered the room was the first to speak. Clearing her throat, she said, 'I've got to say, this is the biggest nightmare of my life. But I do look quite good.'

The other Donna inclined her head in agreement. 'Can't argue with that.'

Staring hard at his other self, one of the Doctors said, 'I just want to talk to you – you, not-Doctor – because I know you're fake. I know that for a fact. So, I want to know why you're doing this.'

The other Doctor looked indignant. 'But that's what *I* was going to say!'

'Well, you should have been faster!' Eyes moving between the two Donnas, the first Doctor said, 'Because that's me, isn't it? Fast? Am I fast? Do I talk fast? Yes?'

The other Doctor snapped, 'But you're a copy of me! You're only fast because I am!'

One of the Donnas threw her hands up in exasperation. 'Oh well, I can't follow any of this. And *that* is *proof!* Cos let's not pretend, I'm the stupid one. And don't argue! That's always been who I am. Ask my mother.'

The Doctor who had most recently spoken looked at her, frowned. 'You think you're stupid?'

The Donna nodded. 'Of course I do.'

That same Doctor gave a half-smile. 'That's very Donna.'

The other Doctor, the one who had asked whether he talked fast, chipped in, 'That's *so* Donna. That's *my* Donna.'

The other Doctor gave him a shrewd look. '*Except…*'

There was a sudden tension in the air. The two Donnas and the remaining Doctor went very still, and stared at the Doctor who had just spoken. Quietly he completed his sentence…

'… Donna does not think she's stupid.'

The Donnas replied simultaneously. One said, 'I do, though.' The other said, 'Oh, but I do.'

But the Doctor who had just spoken was shaking his head. 'No. Donna thinks she stupid. And *sometimes* she thinks she's brilliant. She thinks both. Because that's the astonishing thing about the people from her planet. They can believe two completely different things at exactly the same time.'

The Donna who had said 'I do, though' gave him a beaming smile. 'Brainbox.'

The Doctor she'd spoken to smiled back at her, and winked. 'Earth girl.'

And suddenly the two of them were running

towards each other. They met in the middle of the floor and hugged.

'Oh, thank god,' Donna said.

The other Doctor and Donna strode out from their separate corners until they were side by side. Now they looked like soldiers on parade, formal and stiff. They seemed to stretch a little, to grow a few inches taller. In unison, they grinned. Hungry, terrifying grins.

The real Doctor and Donna turned to face them. The Doctor produced something from his pocket and held it up.

'But!' he said, as if that word alone could hold them in place. 'Salt.'

Donna had been looking with trepidation at the wide, shark-like grins of the copies, but now she glanced at what the Doctor was holding. It was an ordinary glass salt cellar with a metal top. The sort of thing you'd see everywhere on Earth, in a million school canteens, a million greasy-spoon cafés.

'You can't cross salt,' the Doctor said decisively, upending the cellar and pouring a line of salt onto the floor. As he poured, his hand moving from left to right, he said calmly, 'In our universe, it is said that vampires, demons and ghosts cannot cross a line of salt. Not until they've counted every single grain.' He nodded smugly, his expression that of a man who'd outmanoeuvred every opponent to win the best and biggest prize.

The Doctor-copy and the Donna-copy looked down at the thin white line separating them from their real-life counterparts, baffled and unnerved.

'But... that's a superstition,' the Doctor-copy said uncertainly.

'It doesn't mean it's true,' the Donna-copy added.

Still smug, the Doctor replied, 'It's a superstition *and* it's true. Two things at once.'

'You're lying,' said the Doctor-copy.

The Doctor fixed his double with an unblinking stare. His voice became dangerously soft. 'Then walk towards me.'

Donna held her breath. What would the copies do? She could see they were tempted, but also scared. They looked at the line of salt, then back up at the Doctor and Donna. Their bodies – their stolen shapes – seemed to thrum with tension, as if they were building up the courage to cross a high, thin bridge with no handrail.

'Come on,' the Doctor goaded them. 'Stop copying, and make your own minds up. Cross the line.'

The copies turned their heads simultaneously and

stared at Donna with an intensity that made her feel they were trying to drill into her thoughts.

'She doesn't believe him,' the Donna-copy said coldly.

Donna held her gaze. 'But you said I'm stupid.'

'And also brilliant,' the Donna-copy snapped back.

Donna shrugged, tried to sound as scathing as she could. 'Then which one is it, *Donna?* Cross the line? Or count?'

The Donna-copy glared at her, her lips peeling back over her teeth in a bestial snarl – and then, as though compelled, she threw herself down to the ground, dipped her head forward, and began to snuffle like a dog, counting rapidly under her breath as she prodded at the grains of salt.

Addressing the Doctor-copy, who had remained standing, the Doctor said, 'Now, I keep wondering why this face of mine came back, whether there's a reason. But let me say, right now, it was *not* to become you. So tell me, what do you want?'

The Doctor-copy glared daggers at the Doctor. 'You tell us.'

Not intimidated in the slightest by the copy's hostility, the Doctor said thoughtfully, 'It didn't get cold this time.'

Donna looked at him, surprised. 'No, it didn't, did it?'

'Which means,' said the Doctor, turning his attention back to the Doctor-copy, 'you're acclimatising. Your arms are a bit too long and your mouths are a bit too wide, but … are you stabilising?'

'Like they're becoming us properly,' said Donna.

'I just wonder why,' mused the Doctor.

The Doctor-copy echoed the word, drawing it out in a long, threatening rasp. '*Whyyyyy?*'

'Because,' said Donna, thinking on her feet, 'the TARDIS will come back for us. They know that. So if they become completely us … the TARDIS will come back for *them*.'

'But it won't come back while there's danger …' said the Doctor.

'And we'd be the danger. So they'd have to eat us.'

At Donna's words, the Doctor-copy's already-too-wide grin widened yet further.

'Yeah … don't give them ideas,' the Doctor advised her.

'I didn't say eat,' said Donna quickly.

The Doctor turned to his copy again. 'Is that what you want? Escape?'

The Donna-copy was still on her hands and knees, head down, feverishly counting. For a moment it seemed the Doctor-copy was not going to answer the Doctor's question, and then he said, 'We drifted here. In the lack-of-light. Passing no-time. But we would feel it. From so far away. Your noisy, boiling universe.'

The Doctor looked almost sympathetic. Softly he said, 'But that's wonderful. It's a brilliant place. It's astonishing. I could take you there, except…'

'Hostile Action,' said Donna.

'Exactly. If you existed here with no shape, no form, no purpose, then… what's made you so bad?'

A greedy look, a look of relish, appeared on the Doctor-copy's face. 'The things we felt. They shaped us. Carrying across the dark, we could hear your lives of war and blood and fury and hate. They made us like this.'

'We're more than that,' Donna protested.

The Donna-copy suddenly stopped counting and looked up. She sat back on her heels. 'Love letters don't travel very far,' she said scathingly. 'And neither do your lies.'

With that, her jaw extended and her mouth widened hideously, and pursing her distended lips, she leaned forward and *blew*.

The line of salt disappeared, the grains scattering in all directions.

The Donna-copy rose to her feet. She and the Doctor-copy wore identical leering grins. *Hungry* grins.

With no barrier to stop them now, they stalked forward.

Vandeen

The Doctor and Donna took several hurried steps back, until they were pressed against the wall. The grins of the copies grew wider as they closed in.

'*Stond.*'

The metallic voice boomed all around them, and the lights began to flicker again. Simultaneously, the click-click-clicking of reconfiguration began, and to Donna it seemed more rapid this time, more urgent. If the copies hadn't been looming over them, she would almost certainly have leaped away from the wall, fearful of being caught in the sliding, flipping panels and dragged into the machinery.

But she had nowhere to go. Neither of them did. She was bracing herself to throw a punch, fight for her life, knowing it was probably pointless against a shapeshifting monster, when, with a grinding click, the entire wall that she and the Doctor were pressed against suddenly revolved.

She let out a whoop of shock as the wall flipped all the way around. Within a couple of seconds, she and the Doctor found themselves back in one of the dark and dingy conduits that riddled the ship. Escape! Donna was ecstatic.

'That was lucky!' she yelled.

But the wall didn't stop turning. It continued to revolve – and a second later, they were back to exactly where they had started, backs against the wall, facing the copies.

'Or not,' she added as the wall clicked back into place.

Their only advantage, although it was a slight one, was the element of surprise. The copies were clearly taken aback by the Doctor and Donna's sudden reappearance.

'Run?' suggested the Doctor.

'Run,' she agreed.

And before the copies could react, they leaped sideways, haring through the narrow gap between the wall and the shapeshifters, making for the door through which the Doctor had entered the room.

Once again, Donna was grateful that the ship's automatic doors were working perfectly. As they rushed towards it, the door slid smoothly aside, and they ran through into yet another service conduit – or perhaps even the same one they had glimpsed moments before. It was difficult to tell, because this part of the ship was still reconfiguring, the wall panels flipping and sliding and tilting around them. Above the rapid click-click-clicking, like a million clocks all going at once, Donna heard the copies let loose a roar of what she could only think of as bloodlust as they gave chase.

She was acutely aware, as she and the Doctor scrambled through the narrow tunnel, that they had no more than a couple of seconds' advantage. She was aware, too, that their pursuers could *change* – stretch their limbs, increase their stride, and maybe, now that they were acclimatising more fully, even alter their shapes entirely if they wanted to, to become faster, more efficient animals.

Another bellowing roar. Closer this time, and Donna didn't think she was imagining the hint of triumph it contained. She wanted to yell at the Doctor to go faster, but she could barely keep up with him as it was. Every second she expected to feel claws ripping into her back, or a giant hand to burst out of the darkness behind her and scoop her up.

Still, she and the Doctor kept running, their feet pounding the metal floor. Scrambling over yet another raised lip between one section of pipe and the next, she couldn't resist glancing behind her. In the red-lit gloom the copies' contorted, gnashing faces were surging out of the shadows no more than a couple of metres away. She sucked in a breath to yell a warning to the Doctor, but just then the clicking and ticking of reconfiguration seemed to rise to a crescendo. As the sound swept over them like a wave, she saw sections of the wall, like an explosion of copper-coloured moths, suddenly erupt across the corridor in their wake, creating a new wall, a barrier, between them and their pursuers.

Donna let out a sob of relieved laughter, and then became aware that the Doctor was yelling, 'This way!' Turning back, she saw him dart into a left-hand tunnel that may or may not have been there only seconds before.

She followed, just in time to see him reaching a door at the end of the short corridor. It opened, and they stumbled through, both of them blinking, looking around. Donna immediately felt as though she recognised this place, that she'd been here before.

It was the Doctor, though, who was the first to realise where they were. 'But we're …' he said, just as it clicked for Donna too. They were back in the antechamber at the front of the ship, the one that led through to the flight deck. Behind them was the huge bulkhead door that led out into the main corridor.

This time they'd entered the antechamber through a side route – a barely visible maintenance door in the left-hand wall, that Donna realised may not even have existed the last time they'd been here. It appeared they'd been chased up the corridor by the copies, and then chased all the way back down it again, albeit via a different, more circuitous route. Donna was about to ask the Doctor whether this was pretty much going to be their lives from now on when they heard ominous sounds coming from behind the door they'd just run through.

The sounds were a series of rapidly approaching thumps, and they were undoubtedly caused by running feet. The Doctor and Donna exchanged a glance. Evidently the latest reconfiguration had not stopped the copies in their tracks, but had merely sent them on a small diversion. Now, though, they were very much back in the game, and homing in on their prey.

Without a word, the Doctor and Donna raced up the corridor and burst through the automatic door on to the flight deck. The Doctor ran straight to the pilot's chair, dived across it and wrenched or pulled or punched something – Donna couldn't quite see.

The result was instantaneous. A huge, hydraulic shutter, that had been set into the ceiling just inside the door, slammed down like a portcullis, effectively sealing off the flight deck from the rest of the ship. Although edged in metal, the shutter was composed primarily of incredibly thick glass. Looking through it, Donna saw how close they'd come to being captured. No sooner was the shutter down than the copies were crashing into it and bouncing back, having just launched themselves through the automatic door.

Although they had been thwarted yet again, the copies seemed neither angry nor frustrated. Indeed, they appeared positively gleeful to have confined their prey to the bridge. They stood, pressed against the glass, staring in at the Doctor and Donna, wide, malicious grins on their faces.

Donna stared back at them, feeling at first helpless, then indignant, and finally ... *furious*.

Stepping up to the glass to glare at her counterpart, she stormed, 'But *why?* I don't understand *why!* What are they scaring us for?'

The Doctor wandered over to join her, peering with interest at their grinning doubles. Thoughtfully he said, 'Thing is, ten minutes ago, they'd have ripped this shutter apart, got through it easily. Now they're just standing there. Locking into shape. Almost complete.'

That hadn't occurred to Donna. The thought scared her. And that made her even angrier.

'Yes,' she said testily, 'but ... if you'd just listen to my question, thank you very much – why do they want us so scared? If they want to copy us, why don't they just ... sit in a corner and do it? Why terrorise us?'

The grins on the faces of the copies slipped a little. They looked momentarily uneasy.

Noting their response, the Doctor said, 'That's a very good question.'

Donna clenched a fist in triumph. 'Yes! I'm brilliant!'

The Doctor leaned forward, peered hard into the eyes of his double. The copies shuffled back a little, as if wary of him.

'Why provoke us?' said the Doctor conversationally, and raised his eyebrows. 'Unless that's how it's done. The more scared we are, the more the blood pumps. Hypothalamus. Adrenalin. We think faster and faster and faster.'

'It makes us easier to copy,' said Donna.

'Using our goosebumps like braille,' mused the Doctor. 'You're reading us. Is that it?'

The copies stared back at him, said nothing.

'But how do we stop them?' asked Donna. 'What can we do? Stop being scared?'

The Doctor was still thinking, still throwing things out. 'Like the ship. All ticking over. In neutral. Donna, stop thinking.'

She snorted. 'Easy for me. What about you?'

'Just … calm. Just … cool.'

'I am calm.'

'Even calmer.'

She scowled. 'Well, you do it too!'

'I am!' he protested.

Her voice was rising again. 'Stop rattling me!'

A beat. The Doctor took a long breath in, then let it out slowly. When he next spoke, his voice was soothing, almost hypnotic.

'Slow. Slow heartbeat. If we're slow, they can't read us.'

'OK,' she murmured.

'Good. Shhhh.'

For a while, a few months, during the time when Rose had been struggling with her true identity, Donna had tried yoga. It had been Shaun who'd suggested it. It would relieve her tension, he had said. Give her a calm place to go to once a week.

And it had. For a while. Donna had especially liked the fifteen minutes or so at the end of the session, when the instructor had turned the lights down low and urged them to slip into a meditative state. It had been the only time in her week when she had felt completely serene.

She tried to re-create that headspace now. She calmed her breathing. Emptied her mind. Jettisoned all her negative thoughts – all her fear and anxiety.

And she achieved it. Temporarily. She closed her eyes and for a minute or two she drifted away.

But then reality started to wriggle back in, as it always does. She opened one eye, to see her double still standing on the other side of the glass, staring at her.

'How long do we have to do this for?' she murmured.

Next to her, the Doctor sighed. 'Yeah. There is a slight flaw in the plan.'

In eerie unison, the Doctor-copy and the Donna-copy grinned again, as if they had just gained the upper hand in a tactical battle.

'But how can you not think?' said the Doctor-copy mockingly. 'On a ship full of questions. Why the empty chair?'

'Why do the walls keep moving?' the Donna-copy chimed in.

'What are the words in the air?'

'And why did the airlock open and close three years ago?'

Donna saw the Doctor's lips purse; saw his eyes narrow, then begin to dart around the room, searching for answers.

'Don't,' she warned quietly.

'But—'

'Don't.'

'But it's—'

'Stop it!' Her voice was an irritated snap. And with that, the short-lived spell of tranquillity was broken. She sighed.

CLANG!

The sound, metal on metal, was the loudest it had been so far, and seemed to come from directly above them. All four looked up, but above their heads was simply the curved ceiling.

'And what,' said the Doctor-copy with the smuggest of smiles, 'is that?'

'Doctor,' said Donna, trying again, 'stop thinking.'

'But…' He looked at her in frustration, then scrabbled at the sides of his head with hooked fingers '… *Gaaaah!*

He turned and leaped across the room, throwing himself into the pilot's seat. His hands danced across the array of screens attached to it, his eyes flickering up and down and across the scrolling lines of symbols.

'Let me think, let me think, let me think!' he all but snarled through gritted teeth.

Virtually salivating with joy, the copies began to chant: 'Think, think, think, think, think, think, think…'

'What's making that *noise?*' the Doctor muttered, and then his eyes lit up as he saw something on the scrolling columns of symbols that pleased him. Another rapid series of taps, and he looked up expectantly…

The roof began to slide back and down in sections, on both sides, like a huge, mechanical eye opening.

Beyond the roof was a glass dome, an observation dome, and beyond the dome was the oppressive blackness of the starless void.

But between the dome and the blackness was something else.

'There,' the Doctor said softly.

It was a body, drifting and gently twisting, ten or twenty metres above the outer hull. The body was maybe three metres tall, but humanoid in shape, clad in a bronze-coloured spacesuit, that was plated and ridged, like the carapace of some enormous insect.

But the helmetless head, now nothing more than a skull, was neither humanoid nor insectoid. Instead it was long and elegant. Equine. Despite the gaping eye sockets, and the fact that the large, lipless teeth were bared in a macabre grin, Donna couldn't help thinking that this race, whoever they were, must once have been beautiful.

Attached to the waist of the floating corpse's suit was a long, leather-like tether – a safety line, perhaps. On the end of the line was a metal hook, and even as the Doctor and Donna watched, the body drifted closer to the ship, the tether curling and coiling outwards like a snake, and then –

CLANG!

– the hook hit the side of the ship and ricocheted away.

The Doctor clambered out of the pilot's chair and stood almost to attention, looking up, his face set and solemn. 'The captain of the ship. Circling round and round for ever. Caught in the gravity field.'

Donna gave him a puzzled look. 'Caught in the what?'

'Mavity field,' he corrected.

Looking up again, she said, 'But why? Did they throw him out? Her out? Them out?'

'Her,' said the Doctor, and frowned. 'I wonder.'

He turned his attention back to the copies, giving them an appraising look, before stalking across the room towards them. As he studied them, they stared back at him through the glass, arrogant smiles plastered across their faces. But in the Doctor-copy's eyes, thought Donna, was that... could it be... doubt?

'Why is the Captain outside?' the Doctor said. 'Why is she in a spacesuit with no helmet? And why... don't you know?'

The copies stared back at him. The Doctor's eyes narrowed shrewdly.

'I know that face. I know my expressions very, very well, and... *you don't know*, do you? The Captain did something you don't understand. But *what?*'

All of a sudden, the copies lunged forward, pressing their hands and faces against the glass barrier. They looked desperate, ravenous.

'Tell us, tell us, what the Captain did, tell us, tell us, tell us,' babbled the Doctor-copy.

'What did the Captain do? What did she do? What did she do? What did she do?' the Donna-copy ranted simultaneously.

The Doctor stepped back. Then he began to speak, words pouring out of him almost as rapidly as they were pouring out of the mouths of the copies. 'They don't know, they really don't know.

The questions aren't a test, they *need* the answers!' He slapped himself across the side of the head, as if to stimulate his thoughts. 'We're all stuck in the system, because of the Captain. Oh, what did she *do?*'

Blinss

Donna knew that, if the Doctor had one fault, it was that he couldn't resist showing others how brilliant he was. 'But if they want answers, don't tell them.'

The Doctor looked at her, wild-eyed. 'You know what my head is like, Donna. Once I start having ideas...'

And now the Doctor-copy's eyes were flickering too, and his face was rapt, as if information was pouring through his mind. '... then *I* have ideas,' he said, and turned to the Donna-copy. 'So the Captain...'

'... tried to stop us,' the Donna-copy said. 'But how?'

Donna held up a hand. 'Wait a minute. If they don't know why the Captain is outside, then the airlock door, three years ago... that wasn't them coming in, that was her going out. She killed herself.'

'But *what for?*' the copies bleated at her in unison. They looked now like children who'd been denied ice cream.

'She hid her thoughts,' muttered the Doctor-copy.

'So we couldn't see,' the Donna-copy whined.

The Doctor's face was clearing, as answers – partial answers, at least – occurred to him. He grinned and looked back up at the floating corpse with admiration on his face.

'Maximised autonomic brain functions!' he shouted. 'Oh, well done, Captain! Because she knew that even with a lost ship, if it was found one day, if you two ever reached the universe, you'd run riot across the stars. And you were already becoming copies of the Captain – you'd have owned this spaceship! So she ended her life to hide … whatever it is she left behind. Because when she died …'

He turned his attention from the Captain back to the copies, a savage glee on his face. His voice grew mocking as he finished his sentence.

'… you hadn't completed her. So you lost everything she knew. *Gone!*'

'*Ratico.*'

The metallic voice seemed almost to punctuate the Doctor's words, to underline and enhance them somehow. Like dominoes falling in all directions, the wall panels instantly begin to shift once again, to slide and flicker and flip, reconfiguring the interior design of the flight deck so that even the windows started to change shape.

Standing in the middle of it all, looking around, Donna realised there were still many questions they didn't know the answers to. Raising her voice above the click-click-clicking, she cried out in exasperation, 'What *is* that?'

In the deserted main corridor of the ship, with the wall panels ticking and clicking around it, Jimbo the robot once more creaked into life. With a hiss of pneumatics, the machine raised its stumpy leg and took yet another plodding step forward.

This time, though, instead of coming to rest, a further program within the little robot's computer brain was initiated. Squealing and grinding with disuse, the robot's arm slowly rose ninety degrees until it was at a right angle to its body. Then, equally slowly, its thick, segmented index finger extended from its fist, until it appeared the little machine was pointing at something.

Then it stopped, settled. Once again, silent and motionless.

For now.

Sealed within the flight deck, the Doctor was still

thinking out loud. He knew he shouldn't be, but it was a compulsion. He simply couldn't help himself.

'The Captain,' he was saying, 'calm as a Zen master, set something in motion – to stop those two. And she took her own life, so those things – or that thing? – couldn't work out what she'd done.'

On the other side of the glass, the copies no longer wore the expressions of moping children. Now they looked delighted.

'But you're working it out now,' the Doctor-copy said, urging him on.

'No, I'm not!' The Doctor's face creased, as if it caused him physical pain to stop thinking.

'Yes, you are. And so am I! It's all about...' Suddenly the Doctor-copy look inspired. '*Slow*. We can't understand the slow. The Captain set out to slowly stop us. So the ship is slow. The robot is slow. The words are slow. Is that it?'

'Nope!' snapped the Doctor.

'The words move the walls. So the ship is slowly reconfiguring. To become ... a very slow ...'

The Doctor and the Doctor-copy looked at one another, their eyes widening. Donna felt a shiver run down her back.

They know, she thought. *They've worked it out. And it doesn't look good.*

The two Doctors said the word at exactly the same moment:

'Bomb.'

The walls stopped clicking. The panels settled. There was a long moment of silence. Then ...

'What?' breathed Donna.

As if her question had released them, the Doctor and his double were suddenly all energy.

'The Captain set the self-destruct!' the Doctor-copy cried. 'Slowly. So the words are a very slow *countdown*.'

'I said so!' yelled the Doctor, almost as if he was pleased to be proven right. 'I said countdown straight away! It's that simple! Fenslaw, Coliss, Brate means 10, 9, 8!'

The copies turned to look at one another, their faces full of alarm and realisation.

'The robot!' yelled the Doctor-copy.

As one, they spun round, turning away from the flight deck, towards the automatic door behind them. As they took a step towards it, it started to slide open obligingly.

But the Doctor was already moving. He dived for the Captain's chair, finger jabbing at a symbol on a screen ...

And the door slammed shut again, its automatic

response overridden. There was a hefty *chunk!* as it locked, sealing the copies in the space between the sealed-off flight deck and the main corridor.

Now they were all trapped. But for how long? There was a control pad beside the automatic door, and already the Doctor-copy had activated it, and was jabbing and stabbing at symbols, his fingers a blur.

'We're as clever as you now!' he ranted.

On the flight deck, the Doctor was hard at work too. Perched on the pilot's chair, his hands were rippling across screens, his eyes darting, flickering, as he absorbed information.

'So what's got them rattled about the robot?' Donna asked.

The Doctor answered without pausing from his work. 'The robot is the trigger! A primitive mechanical brain that those two couldn't read, taking three long years to walk down a very long corridor, with one slow instruction – *Kaboom!*'

'But the countdown? What number are we on?'

'Ratico!' replied the Doctor. 'That's five!'

Beyond the glass, the Doctor-copy had succeeded in overriding the controls. With a hum the automatic door started to open…

… and the Doctor reached across to another screen, fingers dancing again.

Once more, the automatic door slammed shut.

With a snarl, the Doctor-copy ripped the control pad off the wall, exposing its inner workings, an intricate mass of glass tubes and pipes with liquid sluicing through them. Working together, the copies began to adjust and manipulate, to twist and tweak.

On the flight deck, the Doctor continued to tap feverishly at the screens.

'We can't let them reach that robot,' he said. 'There's only one way to stop them.'

'What's that?' asked Donna.

The Doctor paused, just for a second. Then he gave her a look of such regret, such apology, that a bolt of ice seemed to shoot from the crown of her head to the soles of her feet.

'I'm sorry, Donna. I'm so, so sorry. But the countdown needs to speed up.'

He pressed a big, ominous-looking symbol on the middle screen – and immediately everything went crazy. Alarms began to blare. The lighting dipped dramatically, then changed to a deep crimson that made it look as though everything was soaked in blood.

From overhead, louder and more gratingly metallic than ever, came a single word:

'*Vandeen.*'

Sensill

Saturated in red emergency lighting, surrounded by madly flickering wall panels, Jimbo the robot swivelled at the hips. Creaking like an old castle door, its entire upper body pivoted, so that its upraised finger was now pointing at the wall. It appeared to be indicating the sliding, flipping panels directly in front of it, which were slowly but surely assuming a different pattern. The panels to either side spun away, whilst others dominoed downwards, creating a space.

A space into which rose a panel of three hexagonal grey shapes.

Shapes which looked as though they were designed to be pressed.

'But vandeen is number four!' Donna yelled at the Doctor.

'I know!' he yelled back.

'But we're still on board!'

'I know!'

Further conversation was curtailed by a bellow of triumph from the Doctor-copy. The Doctor and Donna turned to see the automatic door sliding open. As soon as the gap was wide enough, the copies dashed through it, the Doctor-copy shouting, 'Stop that robot!'

The Doctor slapped at a screen in front of him, and the glass containment barrier rose into the ceiling.

'*Don't* stop that robot!' he yelled.

'Could the robot just *wait?*' wailed Donna.

But the Doctor had already leaped past her and was running full-tilt after the copies.

With a groan, Donna went after him.

The next few minutes were all about running.

With the alarms blaring, and the red emergency lighting saturating all corners of the ship, the copies burst out into the main corridor like sprinters erupting from their blocks. Legs and arms pumping, they started running towards the robot, which was so far along the corridor that from here it wasn't even visible.

Seconds later, and about ten metres behind their doubles, the Doctor and Donna leaped through the bulkhead door and began to tear along the corridor in pursuit. In front of them, the Doctor-copy, his legs longer and his frame more athletic than his companion's, was already beginning to draw ahead of the group.

Behind them, the Doctor began to outpace Donna at the same rate – and also, slowly but surely, to gain ground on the Donna-copy.

Thirty seconds passed, then a minute, all four of them going full-tilt – and still Jimbo the robot was not in sight. Suddenly, from above their heads, the metallic voice blared out again:

'*Blinss.*'

With the now familiar click-click-clicking, the walls began to ripple and shift once more. Although exhausted and gasping for breath, Donna somehow managed to summon the energy to yell out, 'That's *three!*'

Ominously, on this occasion, the reconfiguration happened more rapidly than before. Within five seconds it was over, the wall panels and corridor struts moving in a blur, and settling into a new arrangement, coming to a halt just as the Doctor drew level with the Donna-copy.

Before he could overtake her, she snarled and leaped sideways, hurling herself at him with arms extended and fingers hooked into claws.

Barely batting an eyelid, the Doctor made the minutest of adjustments to his stride and deftly, almost gently, took hold of her wrists. Using her own momentum against her, he swept her almost nonchalantly to one side so that she crashed into the wall, and kept running. Not only that, but Donna, a couple of metres behind the Doctor, actually saw him put on a spurt of speed, as if the encounter with the Donna-copy had given him an extra shot of adrenalin.

Still running, Donna now drew parallel with her double, who was sprawled on the floor where the Doctor had thrown her, like an old coat. But as Donna sidestepped to race past her, the Donna-copy twisted, roared, and wrapped both of her arms around Donna's legs.

Donna and her copy hit the floor in a heap, rolling and scrapping. Both scrambling to get to their feet, it was the Donna-copy who managed to heave herself upright first. She loomed over Donna, an awful grin on her face, her eyes like lanterns of hellfire in the crimson light. Her mouth stretched wide – too wide – and her teeth began to lengthen into points.

To Donna, though, who was now thoroughly sick of being terrorised, her double's widening mouth just made a bigger target.

'Oh, this is therapeutic,' she snarled.

And drawing back her arm, she punched her double as hard as she could.

Much further along the corridor, Jimbo the robot, facing the trio of hexagons, unhurriedly extended its arm. Its pointing finger moved closer and closer to the shape at the centre of the panel. It moved to within a couple of centimetres of it.

And stopped.

With Donna and her copy tussling on the ground, the quest to reach the robot had now become a two-horse race. Or rather, a two-Time Lord race, because the Doctor-copy's body seemed identical to that of the original.

Although he was behind his double, and knew that with their matching physiognomies he had little chance of catching up, the Doctor also knew that the Doctor-copy's lead was barely more than a few seconds. There would be very little, therefore, that the Doctor-copy could do to prevent the robot carrying out its instructions before the Doctor caught up to him.

Gritting his teeth, the Doctor continued sprinting for all he was worth.

* * *

As soon as the Donna-copy fell backwards, hands flying to her bruised and bloody nose, Donna was up and running again. The Doctor and his double were way ahead now, but she kept going regardless, in the hope there might be something, somewhere along the line, she could do to influence events.

All at once she staggered, as the metallic voice, above her, boomed out like a clap of thunder:

'*Sensill.*'

'That's *two!*' she yelled, more for her own benefit than anyone else's.

Next moment she was hit from behind by what felt like a battering ram, and she went down, throwing up her hands to stop her face from bouncing off the floor. For now, adrenalin was not only keeping the pain of her bumps and bruises at bay, but also filling her with energy; in a moment, she was able to flip around like a beached fish to see what had hit her.

It was the Donna-copy, of course, her bloodied nose now miraculously healed. Raising her fists to defend herself once again, Donna realised her chances of helping the Doctor were fading all too rapidly.

It was up to him now.

* * *

The Doctor could see the robot.

It was still way off in the distance, but it was definitely visible now. It looked like a small child, in silhouette, standing beside the crimson-hued wall.

Still running, still exactly the same number of metres ahead of his adversary, the Doctor-copy glanced over his shoulder. From his grouchy and calculating expression, the Doctor knew exactly what his double was thinking. Like the Doctor, he had worked out that although he would reach the robot first, it would only be by a matter of seconds – which would certainly not be long enough to divert it from its course. The Doctor wondered, therefore, whether the Doctor-copy would engage him now, try to overcome him quickly and efficiently. Or whether…

Oh no!

Ahead of him, the Doctor-copy's lips curled in a snarl, and then his arms started to lengthen. At the same moment, his legs began to change, to re-joint, to become more powerful, like those of a big cat – a panther, or a jaguar. Almost immediately his body started to swell, to bulk out with muscle in all the right places. He was becoming exactly what the Doctor had feared he might become: a beast built purely for running. A super-efficient speed machine.

The Doctor had tagged it as a possibility, but he had hoped that all the copy's energy and concentration would be taken up by the effort to stay ahead, that he wouldn't have anything left to divert into an act of transformation.

But it was not to be. And as the Doctor-beast streaked away from him, bounding down the corridor towards the dark speck of the robot in the distance, the Doctor clumped to a halt, exhausted.

Knowing he was beaten.

One

Except…

Hoping against hope, watching the Doctor-beast recede into the distance, the Doctor, used to spending long periods alone, began to talk to himself, thinking aloud again.

'But if he runs out of time,' he muttered, 'the Hostile Action ends. And a time machine would know…'

In the sterile, precisely regulated atmosphere of the main corridor, a breeze suddenly ruffled his hair. An impossible breeze. The Doctor turned slowly, a light in his eyes, a look of hope on his face, as a faint sound stirred the air, first rumbling under the blaring alarms, and then gradually rising above them.

It was a familiar sound. A sound both terrible and wonderful. It was the grinding scream of ancient and infinitely powerful engines. They rose and rose, ripping through time and space. Tearing their way back into the here and now…

* * *

Further back along the corridor, Donna and her copy were still tangled together on the floor, scrapping like schoolkids. All at once, though, they broke apart and looked up with astonishment, their fight forgotten.

With a grinding and bellowing of engines, the solid blue shape of the TARDIS was materialising in mid-air. It hovered for a moment, ten or twelve metres above the floor, and then, as it solidified fully, it began slowly and majestically to descend.

It's new, Donna thought. *It's clean, it's mended, it's back!*

What was more, as it floated downwards, it started playing that song again. The one she had learned at school: 'Wild Blue Yonder'. Almost as if it was celebrating its own glorious return.

The Doctor felt like a man reunited with the love of his life after far too long a separation. He ran to the descending TARDIS, and reached it just as it came to a halt, hovering a good fifteen centimetres above the floor.

The sonic screwdriver was still sticking out of the keyhole, so the Doctor grabbed it and pocketed it, though not without giving it a little kiss first. He clicked his fingers, and when the TARDIS doors opened obligingly, he hopped aboard – giving the corridor floor a little push with his trailing foot as he did so, just as a kid does when it steps on to a scooter.

As if it weighed nothing at all, the TARDIS began to glide back down the corridor, towards the two Donnas. The Doctor stood in the open doorway, like a captain at the helm of his ship, his face solemn.

Shoulder to shoulder, the two Donnas ran forward to meet him. As they ran, they gesticulated wildly at themselves, shouting, 'It's me, it's me, it's me!'

Above their heads, the metallic voice boomed out for the penultimate time:

'One.'

As the wall panels began to move again, this time so rapidly that the sound they made was like the whickering of helicopter blades, the TARDIS eased to a halt. Both Donnas skidded to a stop in front of it, gazing up beseechingly at the Doctor. He stared back at them, eyes narrowed, looking not like a ship's captain now, but like the doorman of an exclusive club who was assessing their right to enter.

'It said *one*! The TARDIS translated it!' one of the Donnas yelled, just as, with a last few clicks, the final configuration ended.

Almost simultaneously, the other Donna cried,

'The TARDIS is here – so the number came out as *one*!'

The Doctor said nothing. He just stared at them, frowning.

As the walls re-formed themselves for the last time, the panel of three hexagonal shapes in front of Jimbo the robot's pointing finger, slid downwards and into the wall. The effect was like that of the reels on a one-armed bandit, panels of different symbols scrolling down and down until they finally came to rest.

The last symbol to slide into place, however, was not a symbol at all. It was a big, red, glowing button.

It clicked to a halt no more than a millimetre away from the tip of Jimbo's pointing finger.

The loping Doctor-beast was very close to its destination now. It vaulted the burnt-out remains of the hover-buggy without breaking stride, closing in on the little robot.

Time may have been running out, but it was still a good ten seconds before the Doctor spoke.

Standing in the doorway of the hovering TARDIS, his gaze flickering from one Donna to the next, he said, 'Who was the head of the choir?'

Both Donnas started jumping up and down, like children eager to please.

'Mrs Bean!' they both shouted. 'Mrs Bean! Mrs Bean!'

'And why is Mrs Bean funny?'

His voice was cold, cutting. Both Donnas stopped, flummoxed, their eyes widening, their lips moving soundlessly, as if they were terrified of giving the wrong answer.

The Doctor looked at the Donna on his left.

Haltingly she said, 'Because it's … it's the name of a vegetable? Given to a woman?'

He turned to the Donna on his right. She shrugged, looked helpless. 'It just … is,' she spluttered.

In a burst of movement, the Doctor lunged forward, grabbed the Donna on his right by the hand and yanked her into the TARDIS. It happened so quickly that the other Donna was unable to react. By the time she had thrown herself forward, the TARDIS door had already slammed in her face.

She stared at it in anguish and disbelief.

'*Nooo!*' she screamed.

The TARDIS interior was restored as if new, beautiful and elegant, all icy white and gleaming. The Doctor didn't have time to admire it right now, though. He raced up the sweeping walkway to the magnificent central console, and started manipulating controls – yanking this, whacking that, banging the other into place.

Just inside the door, Donna was slumped over, battered and exhausted, hands on knees.

As the TARDIS engines rose in a screaming, swirling, ratcheting bellow, she slowly straightened up.

Donna – the *real* Donna – couldn't believe what had happened. She stood in the spaceship corridor, alarms still blaring around her, watching the TARDIS fade away before her eyes.

'Doctor!' she screamed, terrified. 'Come back! She's not me! *I'm* me! You've got the wrong one! Don't leave me here!'

But it was too late. The TARDIS was gone. Donna was alone.

The Donna-copy looked around at what would soon be her new domain. It was incredible. Beautiful. From here she had access to all time and space; all knowledge; all forms. She could spread and grow throughout eternity.

But what form should she take? What form would allow her to infiltrate a million worlds, spread her influence across the universe?

She looked at the Doctor, scuttling around the console, oblivious to her scrutiny.

Such a puny creature to command such a magnificent vessel...

Still stunned into immobility, not knowing what to do, Donna flinched as the metallic voice roared out for the last time:

'Tacsladia!'

To Donna, it sounded like the voice of a judge passing the most terrible sentence imaginable.

'Zero,' she whispered.

Tacsladia

There was no reconfiguration this time. There was no need. Bit by bit, the interior workings of the vast ship had been shifting, diverting, reconnecting, its systems transforming in such a way that the craft's primary function had slowly but surely been entirely altered.

But now that process was complete. The ship was no longer an exploration vessel, because there was nothing left to explore. It no longer provided living quarters for a busy and committed crew, because the crew was long gone.

Three years ago, the Captain of the great vessel had had only one option left available to her – and that option was to prevent the entity which had infected and ultimately destroyed her crew from spreading its poison throughout the universe.

It had been a long countdown. A long, long countdown. But although it had been a risk, the Captain had decided that stealth and subterfuge was her only chance of masking her intentions, of preventing the entity from reading her mind.

But now her efforts had come to fruition. Tacsladia-hour was finally here.

The ancient service robot pressed the button.

So this was the end? Even now, Donna couldn't believe it.

She felt the vibration first. Heard a far-off *BOOOOM!* With the ship shaking around her, she felt a wave of heat wash across her from her right-hand side, and turning in that direction she saw a flash of fiery light far, far away.

She had barely registered this when there came another *BOOOOM!*, a little louder this time. Another wash of heat, a little warmer, a little fiercer. And this time the fiery flash that accompanied it was bigger, less a speck and more the size of a match-head.

By the time the third *BOOOOM!* came, this one even louder, even hotter, Donna knew exactly what was happening. The ship was exploding, section by section, starting at the far end. A chain reaction, that would reach her in... how long? A minute? Less?

Shaking all over, thinking of Shaun and Rose, and Mum and Gramps, Donna clenched her fists and hoped the end would be quick.

* * *

It had been almost there! *Almost there!*

When the computer voice blared out for the last time, the Doctor-beast had been no more than twenty strides from the robot. It was so close it could see the button pulsing like a heart beneath its finger. It could see the corrosion – black under the emergency lighting – on the robot's white metal shell. All it needed to do was barge the robot aside, stop it from pressing the button, and the ship would be there for the taking. And with the Time Lord's knowledge, the entity – which had no name, but which had *such hunger* – would be able to pilot the vessel right into the centre of the universe – into the feeding grounds. And there it would gorge and devour, and become fat with knowledge and power. It would *become* the universe and everything in it. And nothing would be able to stop it.

But the Doctor. The Doctor and the Captain. *They* had stopped it. Those puny, limited things, made of meat and thoughts and ideas, had somehow… *somehow*… managed to slow it down, to thwart it. And now… and now…

Twenty strides away.

It saw the robot press the button.

It tried to scrabble to a halt. Tried to change, to realign, to become not solid, not meat, not matter, but what it had been before. Something different. Non-matter. Energy without form. If only it could change back to what it had been it would survive. It would be beyond the limiting laws of this universe.

But it had a brain now. It had a meat-brain, and it needed to use that brain to *think*, to *concentrate*. It needed time to do what it needed to do.

But it had no time. Time had run out. It was trapped.

Still in its Doctor-beast form, it opened its huge jaws in a scream of rage and denial, even as it felt the heat and the fire and the roar of annihilation rush through it. But it felt those things only for a split-second. Because then it was no more. In the blink of an eye, it was roasted into a skeleton, then into ash, then into nothing.

Gone.

The wind howled around Donna, whipping her hair about her face. It was a hot wind, and getting hotter. It brought with it ash and smoke and the chemical stench of destruction.

She saw another section of the ship disintegrate in a boiling maelstrom of fire and light. The sound of the explosion was so loud she had to clap her hands to her ears.

How long? How long now before she was ripped apart by flying metal, reduced to nothing but a memory in the minds of people a billion trillion light years away? Twenty seconds? Fifteen? Ten?

I'm dead, she thought. *I'm dead. And the Doctor...*

BOOOOOMMM!

The blast of hot air almost knocked her off her feet. She blinked away dust and ash and brimstone, and stared straight into the jaws of Hell.

'HADS,' the Doctor said, and with a flourish he flicked a switch, before grinning at Donna. 'Off.'

She didn't respond, just stared at him. He shrugged. 'Please yourself.' He kept circling the console, making adjustments as he went. Eventually he came to a screen, across which swirled a pattern of Gallifreyan symbols. He peered at the screen, pressed a few buttons, peered again.

Then he turned, leaned back against the console, and folded his arms. He looked at his travelling companion, who still stood on the walkway between the doors and the central console. His face was grim, and his voice, when he spoke, was ice-cold.

'Your arms are too long.'

Before the Donna-copy could respond, he leaned across the console and yanked down the dematerialisation lever. Immediately the sound of the time machine's ancient engines, like the trumpeting of a thousand mad elephants, filled the room.

Like the wolf in Red Riding Hood, the Donna-copy cast off her disguise, her mouth stretching wide and her teeth lengthening, as if to devour her prey. Body strengthening and thickening, becoming more monstrous each second, the Donna-copy strode up the sloping walkway towards him. The Doctor, though, didn't flinch. Stepping calmly away from the console, he revealed another lever directly behind him. A brand new one.

Curling his lip in contempt, he reached for the new lever and pulled it.

Instantly the walkway tilted up at the console end, changing from a gentle slope into a steeply-angled chute. As the Donna-creature, caught by surprise, fell backwards with a scream, the doors behind her opened like a huge, hungry mouth.

Donna clung to the wall, which was shaking violently, splitting apart, panels warping and falling to the ground. The next explosion made her stagger, almost ripped her from her perch. This time, the heat that washed over her brought with it twisted lumps of white-hot metal and charred plastic. They flew past her, bouncing off the walls, the ceiling, the floor. Her first instinct was to be thankful that none of the lethal chunks had hit her, but then she almost laughed; she might as well be sliced apart by shrapnel as disintegrated by an explosion in another ten seconds time.

As the sound of the explosion faded, she realised she was hearing things. It was not uncommon in your direst hour, she supposed, to suffer hallucinations – to see and hear things you associated with security, happiness, comfort. In this instance, she fancied she could hear the grinding roar of the TARDIS's engines, coming from right behind her. The illusion was so vivid, so convincing, she couldn't resist turning round…

… to see the familiar blue shape of the Doctor's old ship solidifying behind her.

Leaping away from the wall, knowing the next explosion could only be seconds away, she saw that the doors of the TARDIS were wide open. Next instant, a figure tumbled out of those doors, moving so rapidly that it hit the debris-strewn floor of the exploding ship and kept rolling. Donna had time to register only that the ejected figure was both her and not-her – what Donna Noble might be if she'd packed herself with steroids and undergone some pretty extreme surgery – before she was running. Without a second glance, she raced to the open doors of the TARDIS and threw herself inside.

The Donna-copy, still changing, had been ejected from the TARDIS at such speed that she didn't stop rolling until she hit the opposite wall. She bounced off it, dazed, in pain, cursing the limited meat-form she had adopted. Shaking herself like a dog, she raised her head – to see the doors of the impossible blue box slam shut.

Rising to her feet, she screamed in rage and frustration. But rage turned instantly to terror when – with a cataclysmic *BOOOOOOMMMMM!* – a section of the ship's corridor less than fifty metres away suddenly exploded. She had time only to turn her head before the blast – a tsunami of fire and flying debris with the force of a hundred erupting volcanoes – tore through her.

Like the Doctor-copy before her, she was instantly incinerated.

As soon as the Donna-copy tumbled out of the ship, the Doctor wrenched the lever back up. The walkway dropped back into place, just as Donna – the *real* Donna – dived in through the TARDIS doors. The

Doctor sprang from the console platform and raced down to her, dropping to his knees and wrapping his arms around her just as the shockwaves hit.

Caught in the heart of the explosion, the TARDIS was like a leaf in a storm. It pitched and tossed and spun, batted this way and that as huge, twisted chunks of burning metal, travelling at colossal speeds, ricocheted off its indestructible shell.

Around the TARDIS, the ship continued to disintegrate, blowing up section by section, its myriad pieces spinning and vanishing into the void of starless space. Finally, there was only the flight deck left, a bulbous sphere trailing tendrils of fiery debris, like some cosmic jellyfish.

Then that, too, erupted into flame and was gone. The Captain's body, caught in its mavity field for so long, flared briefly like a match before vanishing for ever. For a moment, the aftermath of the explosion burned bright, and then, with no oxygen to sustain it, it winked out.

What remained of the ship scattered into the blackness in a billion different directions.

At first, it seemed that nothing at all was left. It was as though the silent eternity of nothingness had swallowed up all evidence of the battle that had taken place here. And then, appearing through the dark, came a tiny object. A simple blue box, with a light on its roof that flashed like a beacon. The blue box spun through the void like a lone fish navigating its way through a vast black sea.

Then it was gone.

That was close, Donna thought. *That was SO close…*

She was still crumpled on the floor, the Doctor kneeling beside her, his arms wrapped around the tight, shivering ball of her body. The TARDIS trembled and shook and dipped around them, but they stayed exactly where they were, huddled together.

Neither of them spoke. They didn't need to. They both knew the peril they'd been in. Both knew they'd stared death right in the face and defied it.

But they'd come through. Again. Another battle won. Skin of their teeth. Just like old times.

At last, after an eternity of shaking and lurching, the TARDIS stabilised, settled. The soothing, interior hum of the indomitable old machine reasserted itself.

The Doctor stirred. Gently, he kissed the top of Donna's head. She knew it was his way of saying they'd done it. They'd survived.

* * *

Later, much later, Donna stood by the console, mug of tea in hand. No more coffee for her, not in the TARDIS. She watched the Doctor exploring his new controls at length, taking stock. Occasionally he'd give an appreciative '*ooh!*' like a kid discovering a cool new level on its latest computer game – or whatever it was kids got excited about these days.

Passing a screen, he tapped it with a long forefinger and said, 'She'd almost completed you. That Donna was a 99.9% copy. Except… I thought, "What's wrong?" And it turned out her wrists had an extra 0.06 millimetres. Obvious, really.'

Donna shuddered inwardly at the thought of what would have happened if the Doctor hadn't noticed the anomaly, but she tried to make light of it. 'The devil's in the details.'

He looked at her – and now it seemed as though he too was troubled by the thought of what might have been.

'Yeah. Isn't it just? I keep thinking… I wish I hadn't done that thing with the salt.'

'What, the bad luck thing? But that was just a lie.'

'Normally. Except I invoked a superstition. At the edge of the universe, where the walls are thin and all things are possible. I've just got this feeling…'

His words provoked a proper shudder this time,

her suddenly cold hands tightening around her mug. 'What?'

He went still, as if he was listening. His voice grew soft. 'The feeling of something…'

Then suddenly he was brisk again. Circling the console. Poking and prodding the new controls. Not looking at her.

'Something that's gone. Fine. Good. Onwards! So, anyway, I was wondering. She said… um… on the spaceship. The other Donna. She had your memory. She could remember us, as the DoctorDonna. So she could see my life, and my mind, and my thoughts, for the past fifteen years. All the time that we've been apart, she could remember it.' He stopped and looked at her again. 'Can you?'

Donna shook her head. 'No. It's too much… it's like looking into a furnace. But I suppose she had a great big outer-space brain. She could make sense of it.'

'Yeah, maybe,' said the Doctor evasively.

Knowing there was something he was not telling her, she asked, 'Why?'

He shrugged. 'Just wondering.'

'What did she see?'

'Oh… things.'

'Like what? Come on, where've you been since I last saw you? What's happened?'

He looked uncomfortable now, but tried to mask it with flippancy. 'Y'know. The usual. Robots. Chases. Waterfalls. Wild blue yonder.'

'OK,' she said patiently, knowing there was yet more to eke out. 'But what *really* happened?'

He stopped tinkering. Gave a big sigh. Then looked at her. 'A lot.'

'You okay?' she asked softly.

'I will be.'

'When?'

His reply was deceptively casual. 'A million years.'

There was a lot to unpack there, and she was wondering how to respond, when the central column began to rise and fall, and the familiar bellow of the TARDIS's engines filled the room.

Looking relieved at the interruption, the Doctor cried, 'And there we are! Back home!'

'You timed that to get out of awkward conversations,' Donna said ruefully. But then, as the Doctor operated the door lever, she turned, suddenly wanting nothing more than to see her loved ones again.

'Where are they?' she cried as the doors opened. 'Where's the family?'

153

The Doctor glanced at the readout screen on the console. 'Oh. We might be a day or two out…'

But his words fell on deaf ears. Donna was already outside.

It was the same alleyway! The very same alleyway they'd left a million, billion years ago. Except that now it was daylight instead of night-time.

But look who was here to meet her! Grizzled and beaming and utterly wonderful, with his wheelchair, and his blanket and his thermos flask.

The old man jiggled up and down in his seat, waving his arms in the air from sheer joy. Donna almost expected him to leap up out of his wheelchair and dance a little jig, despite his dodgy hips and knees.

'Gramps!' she exclaimed. 'I said you'd be here!'

'Oh, my goodness!' Gramps cried. 'Donna!'

She threw herself into his embrace, smelling wool and extra-strong mints and that army soap he always insisted on using.

Behind her, the Doctor cried with delight: 'Wilfred Mott!'

Hug over, Donna stepped back – and now it was the Doctor's turn. He threw himself wholeheartedly into the hug, wrapping his long arms – though not *too* long, fortunately – around the little, white-haired man.

When he stepped away from Wilf, he looked rejuvenated. Spiky hair all but vibrating with energy, a big grin on his narrow face.

'Aw, *now* I feel better! Now, nothing is wrong! Nothing in the whole wide universe. Hello, my old soldier!'

Wilf looked as though he didn't know what to do. He looked up at them both from his chair, his hands fluttering, reaching out, to pat first the Doctor's shoulder, then Donna's, as if to reassure himself they were really there.

'I never thought I'd see you again,' he babbled, barely holding his emotions in check. 'After all these years. Oh, Doctor, that lovely face. Like springtime!'

'And Donna's got her memory back!' the Doctor said, laughing.

'Without dying,' added Donna. 'Which I recommend.'

'I knew it,' said Wilf. 'I never lost faith. I said, he won't let us down! He'll come back and save us!'

The Doctor's grin faded. Now he began to realise that part of Wilf's excitement was caused by agitation, desperation.

'Save us from what?' he asked.

'And where's the family?' said Donna, looking around. 'Where's Rose? Are they all right?'

'They're fine, they're safe,' Wilf reassured her. 'I told them to bunker down. I'll keep watch, I said, you save yourselves!'

The Doctor glanced around, but there wasn't much to see. The alleyway seemed quiet enough. 'Why? Is there something wrong?'

As if in answer to his question, a mobile coffee van, unmanned and parked further up the alley, suddenly exploded. The Doctor, Donna and Wilf all ducked as fire, smoke and shrapnel erupted into the air. Then, closer to them, maybe twenty metres up the alleyway, on the opposite side, the service door of a restaurant abruptly slammed open, and a rolling ball of fire surged out of it, accompanied by half a dozen staff in kitchen whites, all screaming and shouting. Not in fear, but in rage.

Even as debris from the wrecked coffee van spilled from the sky and the yelling kitchen staff began to throw punches at one another among the burning debris, another man appeared at the far end of the alleyway. He was a small man, wearing the jacket and hat of a tour guide – but he was going *crazy*, screaming and staggering and swinging his arms, as if fighting off invisible assailants.

Donna's head snapped left and right, trying to process the shocking eruption of what appeared to be random acts of chaos.

'What is it?' she wailed. 'What's happening?'

'It's everything!' replied Wilf, eyes wild with fear. 'It's everyone! They're all going mad! You've got to do something, Doctor! The whole world is coming to an end!'

The Doctor, though, looked every bit as shocked and bewildered as Donna felt. Before he could reply, there was a thundering bellow of sound from above them, and they all looked up.

The alleyway fell into shadow as an aeroplane, a huge commercial airbus, passed over their heads, its underbelly so low it looked capable of snapping off the chimneys of tall buildings. As the sound of it made the very air seem to shudder, Donna got the impression it was plunging from the sky – and indeed, as it soared past, she saw thick, black smoke streaming from its engines.

Then the plane passed, and daylight poured into the alleyway once more. But the relief was short-lived. Seconds later, a massive fireball surged into the sky as the plane crashed down and exploded, no more than a couple of miles away. The windows of skyscrapers shattered; other buildings cracked and crumbled, engulfing the surrounding area in a vast cloud of dust and grit.

As if oblivious to the devastation, the kitchen staff carried on fighting each other, and the tourist guide carried on fighting himself.

Grabbing the handles of Wilf's wheelchair, the Doctor pushed him into the shadow of the TARDIS, Donna just behind them. All three cowered there, stunned and disbelieving, as madness reigned around them.

'What's happening here?' hissed the Doctor. 'What?'*

---

* You can discover the answer in *Doctor Who: The Giggle*

Acknowledgements

For helping me to realise a 50-year ambition, and for making the process so incredibly enjoyable, my thanks go out to Russell T Davies, Steve Cole, Paul Simpson, Gary Russell, Shammah Banerjee, Scott Handcock and James Page.